Jennifer – Jean Francois –
Warning: Contents HOT!
Happy Reading. –xo
Tamia Gore-Felton
7/2/16

The Hottest Summer

Miami's Heat Can't Compare to Summer's Flames

Tamia Gore-Felton

Copyright © 2016 Tamia Gore-Felton.

All rights reserved. No part of this book may be reproduced, stored, or transmitted by any means—whether auditory, graphic, mechanical, or electronic—without written permission of both publisher and author, except in the case of brief excerpts used in critical articles and reviews. Unauthorized reproduction of any part of this work is illegal and is punishable by law.

ISBN: 978-1-4834-5293-7 (sc)
ISBN: 978-1-4834-5292-0 (e)

Because of the dynamic nature of the Internet, any web addresses or links contained in this book may have changed since publication and may no longer be valid. The views expressed in this work are solely those of the author and do not necessarily reflect the views of the publisher, and the publisher hereby disclaims any responsibility for them.

Any people depicted in stock imagery provided by Thinkstock are models, and such images are being used for illustrative purposes only.
Certain stock imagery © Thinkstock.

Lulu Publishing Services rev. date: 6/7/2016

To All of our Hot Summers-
Past, Present, and Future

1

Breaking Up

"What do you mean it's not me, it's you?" I cried, as I gripped the phone. "Trevor, I don't understand how you could do something like this. We've been together since the second week of high school for goodness sake. Doesn't that mean anything to you?"

"Listen, this just isn't working out. I'm sorry if it helps any, I'll let you keep the engagement ring," he apologized.

"Keep the engagement ring!" I echoed. "Keeping the engagement ring isn't going to give me the time I invested in this relationship back. That's ten years of our lives down the drain. Are you sure you just want to throw it all away? What's gotten into you?"

While Trevor rambled from the other end of the line about how he never had a chance to date and have fun; I took off the shirt I was wearing and wiped my face with it.

"But, you don't need to have fun. I mean we can have fun together, can't we?" I blurted.

"Summer, this relationship is a wrap. I'm sorry that it had to end like this. I'll be over to get my things. You can live in the apartment until the lease expires next month."

"What about our wedding plans and the invitations that are waiting to be mailed on the shelf?" I stammered as I thought about the ivory card stock with our names printed in the most elegant cursive font.

"Don't send them out and don't tell anybody else about a wedding because there isn't going to be a wedding."

"Oh, Trevor, you can't be serious," I sobbed.

By the end of our conversation, Trevor had made it crystal clear that he no longer wanted to be in a relationship with me. What in the hell was I supposed to do with two hundred stamped wedding invitations? I lay flat on my back and looked at the ceiling as streams of hot tears ran out of the corners of my eyes. Why did Trevor do this to me? Why did he do this to us? Our relationship was going well, or at least, I thought it was. We'd just had amazing sex three nights ago. Even though Trevor claimed that there was no one else, I didn't believe him. He had to have his eye on someone. I bet his no good buddy Michael had something to do with this.

He'd been acting distant since his best friend moved here from California a few months ago. How was I going to explain the cancellation of the wedding to my co-workers and my family? I'm going to look like a real loser I bet. As much as I wanted to call him back and beg him to reconsider, I didn't. After what he'd just told me, I knew that he was one hundred percent sure that he wanted out of our ten-year relationship. No matter how much begging I did, he wasn't going to change his mind. When he had his mind made up about something he didn't want to do, it was officially set in stone. That was how he was; he was so stubborn.

Thanks to Trevor and his newfound curiosity to live the single life, I wouldn't be a lovely spring bride. The dress I'd picked out and was due to be fitted for was going to go back on the rack for some other lucky bride to wear. The way the dress looked on my chocolate skin made my head spin as I thought about it. Now I really needed a drink, but I didn't have any hard liquor in the apartment. If I remembered correctly, there should have been two peach wine coolers in the fridge. I scooted off the bed only to glance at the box of wedding invitations on my shelf. Seeing the box made me quicken my pace to the refrigerator that wasn't very far away.

The glow from the bulb in the fridge shed light on the dark apartment. I needed to clean this place up, but that wasn't going to happen tonight. As I looked inside, I saw two lonely peach drinks in the corner near a carton of expired milk. I almost gagged because the milk had expired a month ago and the carton was swollen. I thought about pouring the tainted liquid down the drain, but it wasn't hurting anybody sitting in the refrigerator. So I left it there and made a mental note to take it out with the trash in the morning.

After the break up phone call with Trevor, all I wanted to do was drink these wine coolers and get the next week of school over and done with. End of grade testing was a day away, and my overgrown disrespectful students were beyond restless. I was tired of them, and I knew that they were tired of me. I feared that it was only a matter of time before one of them flipped out on me or I flipped out on one of them. Just last week a teacher got punched in the face when he took a student's cell phone. Those teens were crazy about those damn cell phones.

Lately, I found myself asking if I'd made a mistake by getting a degree in education. I loved teaching children. Wait a minute, let me rephrase that. I loved teaching children that wanted to learn. It seemed that all these kids wanted to do nowadays were text, take selfies, and make excuses. I wasn't sure if I could handle twenty-eight more years of this without putting someone's child in a headlock.

With the realization of choosing the wrong career sinking in, I thought back to the wedding that wasn't going to happen. "Dammit," I shouted as my mouth watered. I craved at least four more cold wine coolers when I thought about the money I may have lost now that the wedding was officially canceled. Would I be able to get my deposit back from the venue and the caterer? I needed that money. If I couldn't get it back, I would be out of over two thousand dollars. I should have let him pay for it, after all, he insisted. I just had to be nice and look where it had gotten me. Now I was in a fix. If I didn't get the money back for the canceled wedding, I would definitely have some bounced checks next month.

If we were over, I would have to downgrade my lifestyle. He said that I could live here until the lease was up next month. I wondered if I could sign this lease without him and keep the same place. My credit wasn't the best, but I was going to give it a try. All the office manager could tell me was yes or no. My fingers were already crossed that I would be able to keep this place because I felt comfortable here, and didn't want to deal with the aggravation of moving.

The last time I had my credit score checked was when I got my Honda. That was almost three years ago, and my score was a 646 then, it should be higher now. The interest rate on the loan for the car was high, but I paid it off last year after I received a bonus for being teacher of the year. After thinking about it, it looked like the odds may be in my favor and that I might be able to keep this apartment. Since my car was paid off, I could totally make this work with my salary from school and no monthly manicures, gourmet coffee, or online shopping.

If I still had a car payment, there would be no way that I would be able to afford the apartment. I was glad that Trevor had paid the rent for the month because I needed to start saving today if I planned on staying in this fancy joint. Two-bedrooms, granite countertops, stainless steel appliances, access to a gym, and even a pool were included with the $1,300 a month rent. I'd gotten so used to this place I considered it home, and I barely thought about my mother's shabby apartment that I'd came from back in Miami.

My mom and I didn't have the best relationship, but I had to admit, I did miss her. I hadn't seen her since I'd graduated college two years ago and moved to Texas to start my life with Trevor. I wanted to call her, but I didn't want to hear her say I told you so. She never thought that our relationship would work out, she always said that we were too young for such a serious commitment. I hate to admit it, but my know it all mother was right. I'd probably wait to tell her the news about Trevor calling the wedding off sometime next week. I swear if she said I told you so, I was going to hang up on her.

As I tilted the last drop of the second wine cooler up to the ceiling, I wished that I wouldn't have drunk it so fast. Since I'd thought of my mother, her unbalanced sing-songy voice was now singing the familiar "I told you so" song in my head. With my head beginning to ache, I decided that I would call it a night and searched for my hair bonnet and sleep mask. Neither was far away. My paisley pattern sleep mask was on the nightstand next to the bed, and my satin bonnet was under my pillow. I didn't know why the bonnet could never stay on my head at night. Maybe it was too silky.

I normally took a bath and got my clothes out for work the night before but not tonight. The wine coolers gave me a little buzz, and I thought it would be best if I went to sleep as soon as possible. Since my shirt was already off and laying on the foot of the bed, I unfastened my pants and slid them off as well. Before I put my bonnet on, I went into the living room to make sure the door was locked. I only locked the bottom lock and not the chain towards the top of the door. That way, if Trevor decided to come home, he could enter the apartment without waking me.

My eyes fluttered as I woke up. My sleep mask was still secured by the small piece of Velcro, but my hair bonnet was halfway off. I didn't hear any birds chirping and didn't hear the sprinklers hitting the window like they normally did, which was odd. I snatched my sleep mask off to see that I'd overslept. I guess I was in such a rut after I got off of the phone with Trevor last night that I'd forgot to set the alarm. I usually woke up a few minutes before the alarm clock was due to go off but not this morning.

As I rushed to start the shower, I opened the door to my closet and grabbed my faithful black slacks, a solid color cardigan, and a black camisole. It's May in Texas, and it is hot as hell, but the classrooms at the high school I worked at felt like walk-in freezers. On the list of things that I couldn't stand, being too cold was in the top five. It was so cold in my class that you could see the breath in front of your face when you talked.

Luckily, my slacks didn't need to be ironed, and I jumped in the shower. After drying off, I skipped the lotion, and put on my clothes. After I had pulled my hair back into an elementary style ponytail, I put my glasses on. When I looked at the clock, I knew that I wouldn't have time to make coffee. I had duty in the hallway near the principal's office, and I couldn't be late. I already got in trouble for being late for duty last week, and I didn't want to get on the principal's bad side considering that we were up for pay raises soon.

After I grabbed my keys and purse, I locked the apartment and left. It wasn't even eight o'clock in the morning, and it was already eighty degrees. It was going to be a scorcher today. On my way to my silver Honda, I unbuttoned my cardigan and took it off. When

I unlocked the car, I draped the sweater over the headrest so the leather wouldn't burn my back. I searched high and low for this particular car with leather interior, and I wished that I would have just gotten the standard fabric. The leather fried me to a crisp in the summer and froze me in the winter. After sitting down slowly on the hot seat and starting the engine, I turned the air conditioner on full blast.

I usually checked my text messages now, but I didn't have time to this morning. As I backed up out of the parking space, I almost backed into what looked like Trevor's car. I didn't see him. Maybe it was a car that only looked like his. I gave the car one final glance before I exited the parking lot and headed to school. My mouth watered as I passed by my favorite coffee shop, I wanted to stop, but the line was wrapped around the small building. I hoped that someone made coffee in the teacher's lounge today that was worth drinking. The last time I poured myself a cup, it looked like muddy water and tasted even worse.

I was lucky that the light was green at the entrance of the school, I would've never made it to my post in the hallway on time if it hadn't been. As I stood in the sea of teenagers, I instructed the students to keep it moving and not to use profanity. Just as an overgrown teen with a face full of acne dropped the F-bomb, the principal walked out of her office and called him out by name. I wasn't familiar with this individual and didn't want to be because the attitude he gave Mrs. Frye was downright rude.

When I said, "Good morning" I could have sworn that she rolled her eyes at me as she walked by me without saying a word. At first,

I felt sorry for her because she had to deal with this ill-mannered pupil so early in the morning. But after she ignored me and gave me that God awful look, I hoped he cursed at her some more. I didn't know what was up with Mrs. Frye. She was an angel one day and the devil's advocate the next. No one liked her because she was as phony as a three dollar bill and one teacher secretly diagnosed her with a multiple personality disorder. On her bitchy day's everyone knew to stay out of her way because she'd made several faculty members cry. A few teachers had even walked out on their jobs because of the way she treated them.

Sometimes I wondered what it would be like to be a principal. I bet Mrs. Frye went into her office and did absolutely nothing on some days. Although her salary tripled mine, I wouldn't accept her job if I was offered it today. Just as the bell rang, I stopped thinking about being the principal and watched the remainder of the student's slow poke their way to their class. When I saw other teachers leaving their guarded areas, I moved my feet too.

My class wasn't too far away from where my duty was, so it didn't take me long to get there. I was the infamous biology teacher that all the students talked about. The boys tried to butter me up by telling me how young I looked, and the girls often asked about my natural eyelashes. They thought that they were fake and tried to guess what kind of mascara I used. Little did they know, I didn't wear makeup or false eyelashes. I was never the type of girl to use man-made beauty enhancements.

While my students tried to change the subject often, I never gave in to talk about things that didn't have to do with science. That's how one teacher got caught up and lost her job. She slipped up and said some things about gay rights and her job was gone in the blink of an eye. That would never happen to me because I always thought before I gave the students any type of response. If they were talking about things that didn't have to do with class, I redirected them with a question about science. Some students were always looking for some shit to stir up. But they didn't succeed with their evil plots in my class, besides they knew better.

That's right. I didn't take any junk from any of those snot-nosed teens. I always stood my ground and didn't tolerate nonsense. I'd issued the most F's, discipline referrals, and detention slips for the entire month of May. I didn't care that the kids wrote nasty things about me on the bathroom walls or even if they called me a four-eyed bitch. I'd been called much worse by the parents, they pretty much hated me for failing their kids, but I wasn't going to pass students that didn't do work or turn their assignments in. When the parents found out that I wasn't going to tolerate being bullied by them, they became my friends and pushed their kids to do better. Now all the students have passing grades.

A line had already formed outside of my class as I approached the door from the opposite direction. I always kept my door locked because of the outbreak of miscellaneous stolen goods lately. The nerds were in line first; most of them wore glasses like me. Next in line were the preps and popular kids. The majority of them were looking at themselves in handheld mirrors or applying lip balm of some sort. The pretty boys liked to look at themselves as much as the pretty girls did. Behind the beautiful people were the jocks, all they whispered about in the line were sports, food, and weightlifting. The conversations that I overheard were unbelievable. At the end of the line were a mix of band members, goths, and stoners.

After unlocking the door, I pushed it open and hit the light switch on the wall. "Go in and have a seat. Get your notebooks out because we'll be taking a lot of notes today. Testing starts tomorrow," I announced, as I made my way to my messy desk. A few kids responded by sucking their teeth and the others didn't say anything. They simply followed the directions I had given them. Just because they were following instructions didn't mean that they weren't cussing me out inside of their heads, though.

Just as the bell rang, the last student walked in. Before he could take his backpack off, I asked him to shut the door, and he did. While I set up the overhead projector, I heard a cell phone ringing. After looking up, I immediately reminded the students about the strict cell phone policy and threatened to take whoever's phone was disturbing my class.

"Ms. Barnes, that ringing is coming from your desk," one of the nerds informed me. I quickly stopped what I was doing by the overhead projector and walked towards my desk. As I got closer, I heard the muffled ringing sound. It was my phone ringing from deep down inside of my purse. "Oh, sorry guys. That was my phone," I apologized as I reached into my bag and silenced the call while looking at the screen to see who it was.

"What in the hell did Trevor want?" I wondered. Meanwhile, the morning announcements had come on, and everyone was standing to say the Pledge of Allegiance. I stood with my hand over my heart

as two rude popular girls continued to carry on a conversation. I watched them as one giggled and stopped talking when she saw me looking in their direction. When the moment of silence was over, I informed them that they would both have lunch detention.

After I had written their detention slips, I walked over and handed them to the girls. One took the slip and pouted. The other snatched the slip from my hand and ripped the paper. I was taken back for a moment by the sudden disrespect from the teen. Then I remembered that I didn't want to go to jail today for snatching her little ass up. Without saying anything to her, I walked away and counted to ten slowly in my head. While some students giggled, others watched me carefully with wide eyes and wondered what I was going to do. They knew that I wasn't going to take that as I scribbled a discipline referral with the girls name on it.

2

Gin and Juice

When the bell rang at 3 o'clock, I couldn't have been happier. I was glad that my work day was over. I thought long and hard about taking the next day off after I listened to the messages on my phone from Trevor. He'd gotten all of his things from our apartment while I was at work and left his key on the kitchen counter. I wanted to break down and cry as I locked my classroom and left the building. When I got in the car, I called him back, but he didn't answer the phone. I wonder where he was. He couldn't have gotten a new apartment this fast could he?

On the way home, I stopped by the liquor store and purchased a gallon of off-brand orange juice and a half-gallon bottle of gin.

I couldn't wait to get wasted. I knew that I shouldn't drink and drive, but that bottle of gin was calling my name. Behind the tinted windows of my Honda, I opened the bottle of gin and took a quick gulp. I'd never done that before, and I regretted it immediately. My throat burned like I swallowed a tablespoon of fire. After coughing and looking around the parking lot to see if anyone was watching me, I unscrewed the water bottle that was in the cup holder and drank it. The water was hot from sitting in the car all day, but it made my throat feel better.

Before I backed up, I poured a bit of gin and orange juice in the water bottle and shook it up. After unscrewing the cap, I took a swig. *"That tastes much better,"* I said to myself, as I put the bottle back in the brown paper bag and hid the open container under the seat. When I made it back to the apartment complex, the car that looked like Trevor's was gone. I wondered if it was his car parked behind mine this morning as I gathered my things out of the front and back seat.

I felt weighed down as I carried my school laptop, briefcase, oversized purse, and the paper bag that contained the gin and juice. I had no idea what I was about to see as I struggled to balance all of my stuff and unlocked the entry door. Just as I walked in, the paper bag ripped, and the juice and gin fell onto the floor. Luckily, the bottle didn't break. Before squatting down to pick up my stress reliever, I noticed that the furniture in the living room was missing.

I dropped all of my things to the floor as I saw that the table was gone in the dining area. I couldn't believe it. Trevor took all the things that he'd purchased for the apartment. I wondered if he'd taken his desk too, as I sprinted down the short hallway. After I had opened the door to the extra bedroom we used for a home office, I saw that all of his things were no longer there. My shabby desk was still there, covered with old mail. The imprint from the legs of Trevor's desk was the only thing left that proved something else used to be in the room other than my stuff. If this room was missing all of Trevor's belongings, I wondered how our bedroom looked.

My mouth fell open as I opened the door and entered my room. All that was left was a mattress, a bookshelf, and my chaise lounge chair. My underclothes were scattered at the foot of the mattress along with a few sheets and a comforter. Trevor had taken our bedroom furniture too. Why was he doing me like this all of a sudden? I wanted answers, and I wanted them now.

I dialed his number and let the phone ring and ring. He didn't answer any of my calls, and I left him four voicemail messages. I didn't deserve to be treated like this. Even though he did pay for all the things that he'd taken, this wasn't justifiable. I was going to get to the bottom of this break up if it was the last thing I did. I wonder who had his nose wide open as I looked around the bedroom.

The things that used to be on my nightstand were on the floor by the mattress. My hair bonnet and sleep mask were near the alarm clock and my eyeglass case. When I bent down to sit on the edge of the mattress, I plugged the alarm clock into the wall and set the alarm. *"I wasn't going to be late for work in the morning,"* I thought as I lay back on the only pillow that Trevor didn't take.

I didn't know what else to do, and I was sick of crying, so I decided to stop feeling sorry for myself and clean up. I never realized how messy the apartment was until I started cleaning. How did I let it get this bad? Clothes were piled up in the corner of the bathroom, and there was a nasty ring in the tub too. I wonder if this is why Trevor left me. I was a slob and didn't like to clean up after myself. This is what my mother always used to fuss at me about when I was in high school and even college. I didn't have the knack for organization, and I didn't mind wearing mismatched socks or using the same towel three days in a row either.

That evening, I cleaned the apartment like a mad woman. I swept, mopped, dusted, washed four loads of laundry, and cleaned out my closet. Since I didn't have a dresser or nightstand, I went out and bought plastic bins that look like tiny dressers. They were less than twelve bucks each and would have to work because I couldn't afford any new furniture at the moment.

The new set up would suit me just fine until I figured out if I was moving or not. After I cleaned the bathroom, bedroom, and living room, I faced the kitchen. It was absolutely terrible, and I was surprised that we didn't have roaches. When I opened the fridge, the swollen milk carton from last night was still there waiting for me. I was afraid to touch it and thought twice about leaving it in there. After I found a pair of tongs in the kitchen drawer, I used them to grab the outdated milk. With the carton in the grasp of the tongs I tilted it upside down in the sink and watched the slimy clabbered liquid slide down the drain.

The smell was horrible, and I threw up in my mouth twice before the carton was empty. I cautiously placed it in the trash can and closed the lid. After the milk carton was out of the way, I poured bleach in the sink and the sour milk smell was gone in no time. While cleaning out the refrigerator, I found expired condiments and even a few packets of soy sauce.

I couldn't believe how lazy I'd been as I took three huge bags of garbage out to the dumpster. I couldn't blame Trevor for leaving me if that was the reason he'd left. When I got back to the apartment, I was going to press my luck and call him again. Hopefully, he would pick up this time. After I had got rid of the stinky garbage, I took the long way around the building. As I approached the corner, I saw the car that looked like Trevor's again. This time I walked up to it and looked inside. I saw a box of his things and a gym bag in the back seat, so I knew it was his car. I wondered what he was doing here as I looked around the parking lot.

He couldn't be at the gym because his gym bag was in the car. Just as I walked away from the window, I saw a pretty brown skin girl walk towards it. I slowed my pace because I wanted to see where she was going. The girl didn't go to Trevor's car, she went to the car parked directly beside his and got a box of things out of the trunk. She seemed happy as she rushed back into a first-floor apartment.

I'd never seen her around here before, but then again, I never paid any attention to any of the tenants. With my head full of new thoughts I wondered if this could be Trevor's reason for leaving me. When I got back to the apartment, I called him. I wasn't surprised that he didn't answer the phone again, so I finished cleaning up the kitchen. Before I cleaned off my desk in the home office, I poured a huge mix of gin and juice in a large plastic cup.

Some of the mail on my desk was dated back from a year ago. I was ashamed of myself and wondered if I had a problem. I wanted to shred some of my old bank statements, but Trevor had taken the shredder. I tore the papers the best I could and placed them in a new garbage bag. After sorting through the mail, I tossed piles of junk mail and magazines that I didn't remember subscribing to away. When I was finally able to see the top of my desk, I let out a breath of fresh air.

I carefully slid my desk down the hall and positioned it in the corner since the bedroom was practically empty. After I had gone back down the hallway, I grabbed the arm of my rolling chair and pushed it into my room behind the desk. Then I plugged the cords into the electrical socket and my computer beeped while it came to life. I tried to remember my password as I went into the living area to grab my school laptop, along with my briefcase, and purse.

After remembering the password, I set everything up on my desk and searched for the answer key to the quiz I had given the students last week. I didn't know what I did with my booklet of answers. I hope that I didn't leave it at school because I had to get these grades entered into the system tonight. I looked and looked, but I still didn't find it. I decided to stop looking for them and lay on the mattress for a moment because my head was starting to hurt. I think that I drank too much gin and juice.

While the sun began to set, my stomach started to growl. At that moment, I realized that I hadn't eaten anything all day and that I'd been drinking on an empty stomach. I normally ate lunch at school but didn't feel like fighting with the kids in the lunch line today.

So I skipped my lunch break and took a nap in my classroom with the door locked. As I thought about what there was to eat in the refrigerator, I remembered that there was a box of sausage.

I figured that I'd boil a piece and make a sausage dog with a piece of light bread. I didn't have any hot dog buns and wasn't going back out to get any. After boiling the sausage link, I learned that the loaf of bread was stale, and I only ate the swollen link with a bit of mustard. Now that my stomach was full, I ran a bath in the newly cleaned bathtub. I hadn't taken a bath in so long. I knew that I was going to enjoy this.

When the tub was full, I undressed and stepped into the warm water. I lay back and relaxed before I reached for my body pouf. After squirting a bit of body wash on the pouf, I stood up and slathered my body with the sweet smelling soap. Then I sat down in the tub again and rinsed off. While I dried off, I looked over to my new work area and remembered that I needed to grade those papers and get the grades entered into the system.

I quickly rubbed scented shea butter all over my skin and slid on a robe with nothing under it. I didn't want to go outside, but I had to check the car to see if the answer key fell out while I was driving. After carefully tying the robe, I put on a pair of flip flops and walked into the living room. Just as I opened the door, Trevor and I were face to face.

"Can I come in, Summer?"

I was shocked and very upset with him, but I opened the door wider and said, "Sure."

"It looks good in here," he said as he looked around.

"Yeah, considering that there's no furniture or anything," I replied sarcastically, as I walked back to the bedroom. Trevor followed me and said, "Look, I just came to apologize, I still love you, but I need some space. Can you understand that?"

"Please tell me that you didn't come here to tell me that bullshit," I hissed and sat down on my chaise lounge.

"I saw that you called and had to stop by to give you some type of explanation. Please don't be mad at me."

"You left me with hardly anything. How am I not supposed to be upset with you?"

"I'm sorry, if you want I can have the bed delivered tomorrow."

He then sat down next to me and leaned his head on my shoulder.

"Alright, I won't be mad if you tell me who you left me for."

"It's complicated, and I don't want to get into that right now," he said, as he stood up. Without thinking, I stood up too. When he opened his arms, I embraced him. I wasn't sure if I accepted his apology, but I gave him a kiss.

"Please don't do that," he said as I placed another kiss on his neck.

"Don't do what?" I asked while I untied the belt on my robe. He grew silent as I unbuttoned his pants and shirt.

"So you're just going to rape me?"

"You can call it whatever you want," I seductively replied, as I pushed him down on the chaise lounge. He couldn't resist my sweet smelling body, and he pulled me down onto his lap. As we kissed, the liquor leaked out, and I confessed all of my love for him. When

I told him that I loved him, he replied by telling me that he loved me too.

A thought of reconciliation came to mind as we caressed each other's bodies in the semi-dark room. My breathing increased as he took my nipples into his mouth and sucked on them. He knew how this drove me crazy. I couldn't take it and reached down to remove his erection from his boxers. I made him weak as I dipped his love stick in and out of my warm wet vagina. My nipples hardened, not only because of his moaning, but because of the way I felt. I gave up on teasing him and eased down onto him. With all of his love inside of me, I whimpered as he held me by my waist.

While he bucked feverishly into my goodies, I nibbled on the lobe of his ear. "That's my spot," he whined as he slowed his pace. "I know that," I said, as I moved his hands from my waist and stood up. Then I knelt down and took him into my mouth. I never did this before, and I hoped that I was doing it right. He didn't say a word. He only continued to move his hips slowly. I pleased him just like the lady did her pretend lover in the porn video that we watched last week. My jaws were tired, but I didn't want to stop. If I continued and let him climax in my mouth, this might make him come back to me.

Even though all sorts of spit and drool were coming from my lips, I didn't give up. Trevor's moans turned me on and encouraged me that I could finish this task. When I almost gagged, I wanted to throw in the towel, but I didn't. The finish line was way too close. While his grunts grew louder and more intense, I continued to give him oral sex until it happened. A warm tart liquid exploded in my mouth.

"Damn, Summer. Where on earth did you learn how to do that?"

"From watching porn with you."

"You almost knocked my socks off," he confessed, with a chuckle.

"That's what I was trying to do."

"Since you cleaned up the place and gave me some bomb head, I'm going to reconsider getting back together. You're putting forth an effort, and I can tell that you want this to work." He said as he stroked his deflated erection.

"Yes, I want to marry you. You're the only one that I've ever loved or been with, and you know that."

"Yes, I know that baby, I'll tell you what. I'll renew the lease next month and move all the stuff back in, but I'm going to stay with Michael while you and I take a break for the summer. How does that sound?"

"Does this mean that you're going to be dating other women?"

"Yes and you can date other men too. Think about it. You've never been with anyone else and neither have I. Let's take a break and start fresh with a new relationship in the fall," he suggested.

"Are you sure that you'll still want me?"

"Baby, I'm positive that I'll still want you. I think that this will be a great experience for both of us. Besides, you don't want to get married only to regret you didn't have any fun with your life," he said with a smile.

"Trevor, you make a lot of sense. Let's try it. Just promise me that you won't get anyone pregnant."

"I promise."

After Trevor had left that night, I brushed my teeth and tongue for a full ten minutes. I also used an entire bottle of mouthwash. My tongue felt raw and irritated as I turned the light off in the bathroom. Just before I sat down on the mattress, I looked over at my desk and saw the pile of ungraded papers, and I felt like kicking myself. With Trevor's visit, I'd forgotten to look in my car for the answer key. Since it was so late, I powered on my work computer and inserted a grade of one hundred for everyone. Then I tossed the quizzes in the trash in the bathroom before I went to bed.

3

Mother's Intuition

The next morning I woke up before the alarm clock went off. I was ahead of schedule and back to my usual self. All that was missing was Trevor. I looked over at the chaise lounge and smiled before I rolled off the mattress. *"Last night was incredible,"* I thought as I got dressed for work. I was so happy that Trevor was returning the furniture today. I wonder what he did with it anyway.

Before I left home, I put Trevor's key under the plant beside the entry door because he'd forgotten to take it with him last night. Since I was early, I had time to stop at the coffee shop drive through and order a large cup of hazelnut brew. I licked my lips greedily as the guy handed me the cup of coffee and a small bag that contained a breakfast sandwich. I couldn't wait to get to school so I could gobble this down. I didn't get the green light this morning and had to wait in a lengthy line to turn onto the school grounds. I was tempted to take a bite of my sandwich because the inside of the car smelled like bacon. Just as I took my hand off the steering wheel to open the bag, the light turned green, and traffic moved along rather quickly.

After parking in the faculty parking lot, I grabbed my small bag of food and shoved it into my unzipped purse. Then I put the strap on my school bag across my shoulder, carefully removed the coffee cup from the cup holder, and went into the building. As I was signing in the secretary sniffed the air and asked what I had in the bag. "It's a double bacon, egg, and cheese croissant. I got it from the coffee shop beside the Walgreen's on the corner." "That sure smells good," she replied as I walked down the hallway with my things. "Thanks, I'll bring you one the next morning I stop by the shop."

When I reached the class, I unlocked the door and flipped on the lights. I had twenty minutes to eat breakfast before the bell was due to ring. While I ate, I sipped the coffee and checked my cell phone for messages. I didn't have any; I wasn't surprised because I didn't have any friends. I had a good friend in middle school, but I couldn't remember what her name was. I can remember that it started with the letter "J", and that she was named after her mother and grandfather. My sweet friend moved away right in the middle of our eighth grade school year, and I never saw her again. I always wondered what happened to her, even though I couldn't remember her name, I remembered how she looked.

Her skin was very fair because she was a product if an interracial affair. Her hair was as brown and curly as the hair of a poodle. She was a little taller than me back in middle school, but I grew and figured that we'd probably be about the same height now. I stood about 5'5, and that was with flat shoes on. I can remember her greenish colored eyes and a few freckles on her tiny nose. Now that I thought about it, she reminded me of Freddie Brooks from that show *A Different World*. As a matter of fact, those two could go for sisters.

I missed my friend. We used to talk on the phone and sit together at lunch. She shared some secrets with me that I'd never forget. She told me how she was molested by one of her older cousins and how her mom used to be a prostitute. That's why she didn't have any idea who her father was. Her mother was Caucasian and only solicited men of color. I remember her telling me that every time she passed by an older gentleman of color, she wondered if he could have been her father. I didn't know where my old friend was, but I hoped she found her old man or, at least a father figure.

As I thought about my long lost friend, I remembered being friends with another girl in my algebra class. We clicked instantly and even rode the same bus, but I stopped being friends with her after I met Trevor. That same week he asked me to be his girlfriend, I accepted his offer. I couldn't resist his boldness, I had never dated anyone before and fell in love with his personality. He wasn't that cute, but other girls were crazy about him. That's when I came to the conclusion that I didn't need any girlfriends because I didn't want anyone to steal him away from me.

Back then, I didn't think of myself as being pretty. I didn't look like the girls on the magazine covers or the ones in the music videos. I hated my chocolate skin when I was younger. All the guys at the school I attended only seemed to like high yellow girls, girls that had curly hair or, girls that had hair past their shoulders, and they never gave the chocolate girls a second look. Along with being dark, I had no shape and a gap that I thought was very unattractive. I begged my mother and father for braces, but they said they couldn't afford them.

While the guys at school clowned Trevor for dating a girl like me, he ignored them and held my hand with pride. After dating for nine months, I let Trevor pop my cherry. It happened one day at his grandmother's house when I walked to visit him. His grandmother had a hearing aid and couldn't hear well, so she had the television blasting. Trevor and I played video games in his room until he made his move. I'd never experienced anything like this before, so I let him have total control. After he quietly shut the room door, it happened. We finished the act on his electric blue and black comforter. I was afraid to let him see me, so I left my shirt on and kept my eyes closed the entire time.

After messing around for about five minutes, it was over, and we were back to playing video games on the floor near the foot of his bed. I wanted to talk about what had happened, but I was shy. Needless to say, I didn't say a thing and stayed for thirty more minutes before I told Trevor that I was about to go home. As he walked me through the house, he peaked in his grandmother's room and told her that he would be back in a few minutes.

After waving goodbye to his grandmother, he walked me halfway home and kissed me on the cheek before we parted ways. I was happy to see that neither of my parents was home from work yet as I approached our apartment complex. From that day forward I consumed myself with Trevor, and I hadn't entertained female friends at all. At the time, I thought that he was the best thing that ever happened to me.

When the bell rang, I snapped out of my thoughts and opened the door for my students. They poured into the classroom chatting about this and that while they held on to their number two pencils. As I tossed the wrapper from my breakfast sandwich in the trash, the test monitor walked in holding the end of grade test booklets and scantron sheets. The time had come, and I prayed that my students studied last night.

Following the Pledge of Allegiance and morning announcements, I cleared my throat and said, "Congratulations, all of you passed your pop quiz from last week with the grade of one hundred." Some students pumped their fists in the air, high-fived with other students, or yelled out in excitement. I then smiled as I told them to settle down.

While the monitor handed out the scantron sheets and testing booklets, I drank the final gulp of my coffee and cleared my throat again to read the instructions for the test. Shortly after that, the testing began, I walked around the class and looked over the shoulders of the students. It looked as though everyone had studied and I was pleased with the majority of the answers that they bubbled in on the scantron sheets. Today was the only day testing with my students, tomorrow I had to monitor a class down the hall during my planning period and I was fine with that. With only two more days of school left after today, I was ecstatic.

The day crept by, and I watched the clock like a hawk. It seemed as though the work days were longer because I was about to be free for almost three months. I not only counted down the days to freedom, but I counted the hours too. The feeling of not having to prepare lesson plans, sleeping in, and not being aggravated by students was a feeling I longed for. I absolutely couldn't wait until it was time to pack my classroom up.

When I returned home that day, all the furniture was back. I was so happy that I called Trevor to thank him, but he didn't answer the phone. I wanted to hug each and every piece of furniture as I made my way down the hall into the bedroom. The 50-inch television was back as well, and not only was it on, it was tuned to my favorite station. I stood in the doorway and watched television for a moment before I walked towards the four poster bed and set my purse down. It looked extra soft. I couldn't resist the fluffy pillows and immediately took my shoes off to climb on it.

After removing my lanyard with my school identification and classroom key from around my neck, I reached over and put it on the nightstand. Meanwhile, the actress on television was having an argument with her pretend mother. All the bickering reminded me to call my mom. I dreaded the entire conversation and took a deep breath before I retrieved my cell phone out of my purse. I hadn't talked to her in almost a month and had ignored her calls. I silently hoped that she wouldn't curse me out too bad. Her phone rang four times, and I started to hang up just as she answered.

"If it isn't my long lost child," she said with a bit of an attitude in her voice.

"Mom, please don't start with the attitude. I had a long day, and I was calling to see how you were doing."

"I couldn't be better. I won a thousand dollars the other week at the bingo hall. I was going to send you some money, but you never answered the phone when I called you. The money is gone now. I spent it on a new washer and dryer."

"A thousand dollars? That ain't no money. I couldn't even pay my rent with that. Anyway, I'm glad that you finally won. God knows you've spent enough money at that place over the years; it's about time," I replied as I remembered how she used to neglect me when I was younger and go to that devilish bingo hall. I would come home to an empty apartment with a note on the refrigerator that read: *"Gone to bingo, make yourself a sandwich."*

"I figured that you would say that. It was enough for me. I guess that's all that matters. So how's it going with you and Trevor? I had a dream about you two nights ago, and you were upset. Is everything okay?"

I almost went into shock when I heard that. I guess it was a mother's intuition or something. Mom was right on the money because a few nights ago, I was in bed crying my eyes out and drinking my last two wine coolers.

A lie spilled from my mouth with ease, and I replied, "Things are going great. I'm doing well, and so is Trevor."

"The two of you proved me wrong. I never thought that you guys could make this high school sweetheart thing last so long. I guess Trevor is a good guy after all," she confessed.

I changed the subject and crossed my fingers that she wouldn't ask about the wedding while I changed the subject.

"We only have a few more days of school left, and I'll be out of work for a while. I can't wait for summer vacation."

"You should visit me in Miami. I'd love to have you. I haven't seen you in about two years, besides there's someone I want you to meet."

I ignored the whole someone I'd like you to meet part of her statement and replied to the part about visiting this summer.

"Mom, I don't know. Trevor still has to work during the summer months, and his availability isn't as flexible as mine. We may decide to go somewhere, but it will probably only be for a weekend. I'll let you know if we decide to come to Miami," I fibbed.

"We? If he can't bring his narrow behind to Miami to visit then you come alone. You guys aren't connected at the hip are you?"

"No ma'am, we're not."

"That reminds me. Summer, where on earth is my wedding invitation? The two of you are still getting married aren't you?"

My stomach dropped before I replied, "Of course, we are Mom. I'll mail them out soon. The place that printed the first set of invitations made a mistake, so they have to print a new set."

"Oh, well make sure they are perfect, you can't send out invitations with mistakes on them. The people would really be talking then."

"Yes, they would be," I agreed as I exhaled.

By the time I got off the phone with my mother, I wanted to scream. I regretted calling her because she asked too many damn questions. I couldn't believe that I made up a lie that fast about the wedding invitations. I didn't like lying, but I wasn't ready to tell her about the separation. I feared that my blood pressure was up because my mother had done the running man on my last nerve. The only way I could relieve my stress was with sex or with a nice stiff drink, and since Trevor wasn't answering his phone, I fixed a cup of gin and juice.

After taking a few sips, I put the cup back in the refrigerator and decided to make a grocery store run. As soon as I walked to the parking lot, I looked around and saw Trevor's car. It was parked in front of the apartment that the pretty girl came out of the other evening. *"Something had to be going on between the two of them."* I thought to myself, as I looked in my car for some garbage to take to the dumpster in the rear of the apartment complex.

When I realized that I didn't have any. I was forced to go back upstairs and gather garbage from my apartment. Considering that I'd cleaned up yesterday, I didn't have much trash in the house and took the bag out of the trash can in the kitchen anyway. It was mostly filled with air, but nobody knew that except for me, so I headed back outside and took the long way around the building. After I tossed the bag in the dumpster, I walked closer to the terraces on the backside of the apartment complex. As I walked by kitchen windows, patio sets, and grills, I looked around to see if anybody was watching. Since I was the only one behind the building, I stopped when I got to the brown girl's kitchen window, which was directly over the kitchen sink. The blinds were not only open, but her window was up.

As I peered inside, I noticed that her kitchen was identical to ours. I figured that the layout was too, but I could only see a little of the living room area. The aroma that I smelled took my mind off of the layout of the apartment. Something delicious was cooking. The food smelled so good that my stomach started to growl. When I heard talking, I ducked down underneath the window.

"Are you sleeping over tonight?" She asked.

"Most definitely, I couldn't get you out of my mind all day," I heard Trevor say.

"I couldn't wait for you to get here, and I can't wait for you to see what I have planned."

"What do you have planned?" He questioned.

"I can give you a preview now if you'd like."

I didn't hear any talking after that. I only heard a few footsteps and lip smacking. Before I peeped in the window, I'd already known that they were kissing, but I just had to see. As she kissed Trevor, her hands rubbed his chest, and she moved them lower until she reached his belt buckle. While she fumbled with his belt, my mouth got dry, and I ducked down a little. My thoughts raced as I heard his zipper come undone and Trevor start moaning. Without looking in the window again, I duck walked from underneath it and stood up. I had seen enough and I'd heard enough.

Obviously, Trevor had been seeing this girl for some time. I knew she wouldn't drop down to her knees and suck him off on the first date or even the second date. But, then again, I didn't know what sort of home training this chick had. Sucking guys off could have been one of her favorite hobbies for all I knew.

After I had walked around the building, I got in my car and called Trevor. Needless to say, he didn't answer the phone. On the way to the grocery store I tried to remember what I needed to shop for, but my mind only went back to Trevor. I wondered if he'd climaxed yet. As I almost ran a red light, I slammed on the brakes. I had to stop thinking about him. Maybe it would be a good idea to get away for a while. Going to Miami didn't sound like a terrible idea anymore.

At the grocery store, I only bought enough food to last for the next three days. If I was going to go to Miami, I wouldn't need to stock up on food. I only got bread, sandwich meat, sliced cheese, eggs, sausage, wine coolers, and a frozen pizza. As I walked around the produce section looking for a bottle of wine, the produce guy eyeballed me. He was very handsome and had a lot of muscles. For some reason, I wondered if he had more to offer than Trevor. I walked over near the oranges to get a closer look at him and took a peek at his name tag. His name was Mark.

While he rearranged fruit, I checked him out from every angle. The brother looked like he had it going on. Just as I was about to pick up a bag of oranges, he said, "Can I help you with something?" I was startled because I wasn't expecting him to say anything.

"Uh, I was wondering if you'd like to join me for drinks one evening at my place." I shyly said as I put the bag of oranges in my shopping cart.

"This isn't a joke is it?"

"No, it isn't. I think that you're very attractive, and I'd like to get to know you. Forgive me if I'm coming on too strong."

"I can't believe this. I must be dreaming." He said with a chuckle and then added, "That sounds great. My name is Mark."

"Hi Mark, my name is Summer. Nice to meet you."

After talking to him for twenty minutes, I walked away with his phone number and a smile on my face. I couldn't believe that I'd just done that. What on earth had gotten into me? I guess it didn't matter because I had his phone number and he had mine. While I waited in line, I took the bag of oranges out the buggy and sat them on the rack with the overpriced bags of potato chips. The lady behind me looked at me and asked if she could have the bag of oranges and I picked them up and handed them to her.

After I left the grocery store, I went back home. I couldn't resist, I had to see if Trevor's car was there, and it was. After satisfying my curiosity, I rolled my eyes and gathered the grocery bags from out of the trunk. Back in the apartment, I put away the grocery that I'd just purchased. The refrigerator still looked empty, but that was okay. I thought that I had lost my appetite after seeing Trevor with that woman, but to my surprise, I wanted to eat.

I debated about eating a sandwich or popping the frozen pizza in the oven. I figured that a few slices of pizza would go great with an ice cold wine cooler or the chilled gin and juice that I'd left in the freezer. Just as I popped the pizza in the oven and set a timer, my cell phone rang. I raced to my purse and dug for my phone thinking that it was Trevor calling. When I didn't see Trevor's name on the screen of the phone, I wondered who in the hell this was.

"Hello," I answered dryly.

"Hey, Summer, this is Mark."

Damn, it had slipped my mind that fast that I had given him my number.

"Oh, Hi Mark. Are you off of work already?"

"No, I get off at eleven. I'm taking a little break. You weren't busy were you?"

"No, I just put a frozen pizza in the oven, it won't be done until twenty-five minutes or so. What's up?"

"I just wanted to tell you that I can't believe you asked me for my number. I've seen you in the store often and wanted to ask you for yours, but I always seem to chicken out."

"Really?"

"Yes, you're so pretty. I guess that I was afraid of being rejected."

I blushed a little before I asked, "So, when are you going to be able to come over?"

"I'm free this Friday evening after six, would that be a good time for you?"

"Yes, that will be perfect."

"Do you want me to bring anything? Are we just going to drink?"

"You can bring whatever your heart desires."

"Alright, that sounds great. I may give you a call tomorrow morning if that's okay."

"I'll be working. How about I give you a call on my break tomorrow."

"I'd like that," he said.

After talking for a few more minutes, he had to go. I felt refreshed as I sauntered to the kitchen and looked in the oven at the pizza. It felt good talking to someone on the phone other than my mother and Trevor. I wished that I had more friends to talk to, that way I wouldn't be thinking about you know who all the time.

Trevor wasn't only my first love. He was my first lover. I'd never dated anyone, talked on the phone to any other guys, or even kissed someone else. This was going to be hard for me. I hoped that going back to Miami for a while would be an unforgettable experience. I needed some excitement in my life, but most of all I needed to get Trevor out of my head. With him messing around with a girl in the same apartment complex that I lived in, I knew I had to get away.

The last few days of school flew by, and words couldn't express how happy I was. It was finally Friday, my classroom was spotless, and all of my grades were turned in for the year. As I locked the door of my room, Mrs. Frye walked up to me and said, "We appreciate all you do for our students and school," then she gave me an awkward hug. "Oh, thank you. Mrs. Frye." "You're very welcome, Ms. Barnes.

Oh, I'm still waiting for an invitation to your wedding," she said with a smile as she walked away.

I guess that she was in a great mood today. Hell, who wouldn't be? It was the last day of school, the weather was fantastic, and I just remembered that I had a date with Mark tonight. I hurried down the hall as I waved goodbye to a few faculty members. "Have a great summer," I yelled, as I flashed a smile. I tore into the envelope as soon as I busted through the entry doors of the office. Inside was a pair of movie tickets and a gift card to the Applebee's uptown. This was a sweet gesture, and I wondered if all the teachers got the same gift cards. Ah, what did I care? I was going to use these tickets and gift card for me and Mark's first date.

As I got in the car, I called Mark and asked him if he wanted to have dinner and possibly catch a movie. He agreed, and I headed home to get ready. This time, when I pulled into the parking lot, I didn't look for Trevor's car. I didn't care if he was visiting with his new girlfriend because I was going to get to know Mark better tonight.

4

Ego Trip

I didn't think that I'd get frisky with Mark tonight, but I wasn't sure, so I shaved just in case. I wasn't sure of what to wear either and debated on jeans or a skirt. Since it was hot outside, but freezing cold in the movie theaters and restaurants, I chose the jeans. I paired the dark denim with an olive colored shirt that complimented my complexion; then I switched purses. I didn't feel like lugging my huge sack of a pocket book around tonight. Tonight I would wear a purse that looked like a coconut. My mother had purchased it at a yard sale for me a very long time ago.

Not only was the purse small, but it was adorable, and I was sure that it would make an interesting conversation piece if I ran out of things to talk about with Mark. After fishing out the necessities in my old purse; I transferred my lip balm, hand sanitizer, cell phone, change purse, and a few peppermints inside of the shell like purse. After I was fully dressed, I looked in the mirror at my face without my glasses. I wished that I could go without them tonight, but considering that my night vision sucked, I knew that wouldn't be a good idea.

I put them on and considered scheduling an appointment at the eye doctor sometime soon. I wondered how I would look with contacts instead of the glasses. The girl that Trevor was with didn't wear glasses, but then again, I'd only seen her twice. So I wasn't sure if she'd worn glasses or not, either way, my mind was made up and it was time for my glasses to go. After I had turned the bathroom light off, I grabbed the coconut purse off the bed and left the apartment. In the parking lot, I heard some loud arguing coming from the end of the sidewalk. When I looked in that direction, I saw an older woman fussing at her teen son. From what I heard, he'd taken her car without her permission and used all of her gas. Before she pulled out her belt, I got in my car and left because I didn't want to witness child abuse or any other crime.

When I reached Applebee's, I called Mark. He said that he was already parked in a white 4x4. My eyes searched the packed lot until they found his white pick-up truck. I then cautiously pulled out of my parking space and pulled up next to him. Before I got out of the car, I reached into the glove box for the gift card that Mrs. Frye had given me earlier. After I got out of the car, I stuffed the card into my back pocket and locked the doors.

Surprisingly, he greeted me with a hug. "Hey, it's so good to see you again." "It's good to see you too," I replied. It felt unusual hugging someone else, and his body was so different from Trevor's. I felt his muscles as soon as he leaned into me. In the back of my mind, I wondered if he was a health nut. On top of feeling good, he smelled good too. He had on just the right amount of cologne. The fragrance smelled so good that I wouldn't mind wearing some of it myself.

As we approached the door to the restaurant, he held it open for me. I liked that he did that. *"So far so good,"* I thought as the hostess opened the next set of doors for the both of us. I couldn't believe my eyes when we walked in. I spotted not four, but five of my coworkers seated at the bar. I guess that Mrs. Frye did give all the teacher's the same gift cards. I didn't really know these teachers because I didn't interact with them every day, but I did know all of their names. From the looks of things they all were getting their drink on. I guess they were happy about the last day of school too. The five of them had so many shot glasses and beer bottles in front of them that I wasn't worried about them seeing me. They probably couldn't even see the person that was sitting next to them due to all the smoking going on.

Before the hostess seated us in a booth near the bar, I took my last breath of fresh air as we walked through a cloud of smoke. I didn't want to sit here, but the only other available seats were right beside our booth.

"This place is jam packed."

"Yeah, I know. I see a few of my coworkers over there," I replied as I looked at the menu.

"So what are you going to order? Do you have a taste for anything in particular?"

"I'm not sure. Maybe just an appetizer and a few drinks. Oh, I forgot to ask you. What kind of liquor do you prefer?"

"Hennessy. I love a good stiff drink," he replied while closing the menu.

"Will you be drinking tonight?"

"I'm not sure. Why, are you trying to get me drunk or something?"

As I laughed, the waitress came and took our drink order. I ordered a glass of water and a fruity sangria. Mark only ordered a glass of water with no ice. Just as the waitress walked away, I said, "No, I'm not trying to get you drunk. I was just curious. By the way, what's up with ordering your drink without ice?"

"My teeth are a little sensitive."

"That must suck," I blurted.

"I'm used to it. My teeth have been like this since I was little. One summer I stayed with my grandmother, and she let me and my brother eat all the ice pops we wanted. My brother and I used to have these contests, whoever finished eating their ice pop first would be able to sleep on the top bunk. I won every time because I always chewed my ice pops."

"Oh, my goodness. Are you serious?"

"Yes, I don't even walk down the ice cream aisle at work," he admitted with a serious face.

"It sounds like your grandmother had the two of you spoiled."

"Spoiled wasn't the word," he answered as the waitress returned.

"Are you guys ready to order?" She asked with a pen and pad of paper in her hand. I wasn't because I'd been looking into Mark's brown eyes as he talked to me.

"Yes, I'll take an order of hot wings for my appetizer and the bacon cheeseburger with extra pickles and fries for my meal," Mark confirmed.

"I'd like to order the mozzarella sticks and that's all. You can bring them out for my meal," I told the waitress as I slid my menu to her.

After the waitress walked away, she soon returned with our drinks. I sipped my sangria slowly as Mark opened up to me. He was twenty-nine and had been in the military for the past ten years. He got out of the Army three months ago and started working at the grocery store. When he was in high school, he used to work at the store and transitioned back into the job as soon as he returned home. I felt a little better about his job situation when he told me that he had an interview at the police department scheduled.

I'd hardly said a word and listened inquisitively as he talked. When the waitress brought our food, I smiled until I saw one of my coworkers standing behind her. "Excuse me, ma'am," she said as she left our table to greet some new customers. Elizabeth sat down beside me and said, "Summer, aren't you going to introduce me to your fiancé? He's very handsome." I could tell she was drunk, so I tried to brush her off.

"Elizabeth, what in the world are you talking about? I don't have a fiancé."

"Well, I heard through the grapevine that you are indeed getting married, and I want an invitation. You're going to be such a lovely bride."

"I'm sorry, but the grapevine gave you the wrong information. They must've been talking about the other teacher named Summer. The one that teaches the seniors possibly."

"Nope, I am certain that it's you. I want my invitation young lady," she announced as she got up and staggered back towards the bar.

While Mark and I watched her almost fall off of a stool, a few of the other teachers waved in our direction. After I had waved back, I turned back around, and Mark looked at me. Before he could ask me if there was any truth to what Elizabeth said. I blurted, "They always confuse me with this other teacher named Summer. Don't you think if I were getting married, I'd know about it," I joked as I took a big gulp of my sangria.

I excused myself to go to the restroom when we were both done eating. I didn't have to pee, but I made like a lemon and squeezed anyway. While a steady stream of urine came out, I shook my head as I thought about Elizabeth. *She hardly talks to me at school. Why in the hell would she say something to me tonight?* After I was finished in the stall, I washed my hands in front of the mirror and unzipped my coconut purse. My lips were a little dry and I needed to apply some lip balm. I figured that now was the perfect moment to reapply because we were about to leave the restaurant and Mark may try to kiss me.

When I returned to the booth, he had already paid the bill. After telling him about my gift card, he said that we could use it the next time we came to Applebee's. I guess that meant that there was going to be a second date. Mark held the door open for me as we left the restaurant. "Did you still want to go to the movies?" He asked as I looked at my watch.

"Damn, the movie started thirty minutes ago. I guess we'll have to go another time."

"That's fine with me," he said.

"Well, I suppose that means our date is over then."

"Yes, it does, but we can go out again soon."

I kept a straight face even though I wanted to frown. I wasn't ready for our date to end. I hated that I didn't keep an eye on the clock, and we missed out on going to the movie theater tonight. Maybe this was a good thing, the last thing I wanted to see when I got to the theater was more of my coworkers.

"I enjoyed myself Summer. Call me and let me know that you made it home okay." As he moved in closer, I pressed my moist lips together. I thought for sure that he was going to kiss me, but he didn't. He gave me another hug and opened the car door for me after I unlocked it.

On the drive home, I thought about how bad I wanted him to kiss me. *"Maybe I should've just kissed him,"* I thought. Even though he'd only hugged me briefly, the smell of his cologne was on my blouse. My nipples grew harder as the masculine smell filled my nostrils. I wished that I had a man to lay with tonight, I wondered where Trevor was until I pulled into the apartment complex lot and saw his car parked at the other end. He was probably getting it on with the pretty brown girl.

When I got into my apartment, I locked both locks and left a trail of clothes from the front door to the bedroom. Before I climbed on the bed, I set my coconut purse on the nightstand and put on my sleep mask. Since there was no school tomorrow, I didn't bother to put on my bonnet and got comfortable under the covers. A part of me wanted to watch television, but I decided not to.

My thoughts were on Trevor and I wanted him here with me tonight more than ever. As I turned over I realized how much I hated sleeping alone and fell into a light sleep within minutes. I was startled out of my slumber when my cell phone rang from inside of my purse. Right away, I knew that it was Mark because I'd forgotten to call him.

I quickly removed my sleep mask and reached for my purse to retrieve the ringing phone. I looked at the screen with blurred vision and answered, "I'm sorry, I made it home. I just climbed in the bed."

"Great, I just wanted to make sure you were safe," Mark said.

"That's awfully sweet of you. I appreciate that. Did you make it home yet?"

"No, I'm almost there, though."

"I can talk to you until you get there if you want me to."

"Alright, I'd like that."

That night Mark and I chatted on the phone until the sun came up. I lost track of time and couldn't believe what time it was when I looked at the clock. When we finally said good morning to each other and hung up it was almost seven a.m. I didn't know how he was going to function at work today. He had to go to work at eleven. As I fluffed my pillow and pulled my sleep mask down over my eyes,

I thought about going to see him at the store today. But it wouldn't be until later, much later. I had some sleep to catch up on.

I slept until a little after one in the afternoon and felt refreshed. It's funny, but the first thing on my mind when I woke up was Mark. I wondered if he was having a good day at work or if he'd fallen asleep in a box of bananas. As I kicked the covers off I regretted not taking a shower last night when I got home from the restaurant. Not only did my hair smell like smoke, but so did my sheets. That second hand-smoke wasn't anything to play with. As much as I didn't want to wash my hair, I did while I showered.

When I was finished, I blow-dried my hair in front of the mirror without my glasses. Seeing myself without my extra set of eyes made me remember to schedule an eye exam. I wondered how I would look with contacts and was a little afraid of taking something in and out of my eyes. After my hair was dry, I applied a small amount of moisturizer to my scalp and styled it. My hair didn't look bad, but I needed to schedule an appointment at the salon soon. The ends looked a bit dry after using the high heat setting on the blow dryer today.

Since I already knew that it was hot outside, I put on a pair of ripped shorts that I still had from college. The shorts weren't too short. However, they did have a lot of rips and tears in them. While I thought about the possibility of one of my students seeing me in these shorts, the thought of tossing them in the garbage came to mind. That's when I made my mind up. I was going to wear my old shorts, and that was that, if any of my students saw me they would just see me.

I then threw on a white fitted tank top and a pair of tan sandals. I was on my way out the door until I noticed that I didn't have my purse. It wasn't on the nightstand. As I looked around the bed, I wondered why I was thinking about my students. Today was the official first day of summer break, and those knuckleheads should have been the last thing on my mind.

My purse was under the bed. It had rolled off of my nightstand. After I had made sure that nothing had fallen out, I put the strap on my shoulder and locked the apartment. When I reached the parking lot, I was tempted to look for Trevor's car, but I didn't dare look. On my way to the grocery store, I called the eye doctor to schedule an appointment and luckily they had an appointment available today. I happily confirmed the four thirty time slot as I looked at the clock to see what time it was. It was only three, so I had time to visit Mark.

When I walked into the grocery store, I headed towards the produce department and spotted him arranging bags of salad mix.

"Hey, Mark."

When he heard my voice, he looked up and smiled.

"Hey, doing more grocery shopping today?"

"Nope, I only came by to see you. I had to make sure that you weren't sleeping on the job."

He let out a laugh and then answered, "No. I'm alright. I was going to call you on my break to see if you wanted to hang out tonight because I'm off tomorrow."

"That sounds great. So are we going to Applebee's again? You know that I still have that gift card," I reminded him.

"No. No Applebee's tonight. How about we go to the movies and decide on where we'll eat afterwards."

"That sounds like a plan."

"So what are you up to today? I love those shorts by the way. You look beautiful."

I blushed before telling him about my eye doctor's appointment and thanked him for the compliment.

"You're welcome. I'll call you as soon as I get off."

"Okay, if I don't leave now, I'll be late for my appointment. I better get going."

"Yeah, I'd better get back to work too. Thanks for stopping by, you brightened up my day."

"You're welcome. Don't forget to call me."

"I won't forget. I promise," he replied as I walked away.

Seeing Mark did something to me, I felt strange. I think I wanted to have sex with him. On the way to my eye exam, I wondered how his body looked and if he could hold a candle to Trevor in the bedroom. I smiled to myself as I parked and went inside the doctor's office. The appointment didn't take long, and I decided that I would try something new. After the doctor had checked my eyes, he informed me of the different kinds of contacts and showed me a pamphlet with all the different colors that were available.

I'd always wondered what I would look like with different color eyes. My eyes were black. I never knew that there were so many colors to choose from either. There were shades of gray, purple and even a teal color along with the regular blues, browns, blacks, and greens. I liked the hazel color and decided to order a month's supply along with several clear pairs. I just wanted to see how they would look, if I didn't like them, I would go back to wearing my glasses.

Before I left the receptionist told me that my order would be available for pick up at noon, the following Monday. I was so excited about my new eyes that I didn't know what to do. I smiled as I headed back home only to see Trevor and his new girl unloading furniture into her apartment. *"I guess she was here to stay,"* I thought as I pretended like I didn't see him. He looked my way, but I don't think his girl saw him. *"I don't know why the hell he's looking in my direction. He's the one who wanted space,"* I mumbled as I unlocked the door to my apartment.

The perspiration that had gathered on the bridge of my nose dried up as I entered the apartment. It was cool and dark in here, just the way I liked it. I had a few hours until Mark was due to get off of work, so I used the time to straighten up and picked out an outfit to wear to the movies. As soon as the clock struck seven, he called.

"Did you decide on a movie yet?" He asked after I answered the phone.

"I knew that I forgot to do something. I didn't even check. Would you like to watch a movie at my house? I can go to the Redbox and get something real quick."

"Okay, that sounds good. Do you know what you want to eat or at least what you have a taste for?"

"Nope, I haven't the slightest clue," I replied with a giggle.

"Let me go home and take a shower, I should make it to your place by 8:30 at the latest. If you get the movie, I will bring some food."

"That's sounds good to me. I live in Penelope Terrace, in apartment 3B. It's right off of Sunset Avenue."

When I got off of the phone, I went to the Redbox that was around the corner at Walgreen's. After selecting a movie that I'd never heard of, I went inside the store and purchased a bottle of wine and a box of condoms. *"I'd rather be safe than sorry,"* I said to myself as the friendly cashier checked me out. When I pulled back into the parking lot at the apartment complex, I didn't see Trevor. The furniture truck was still there, but he and his new boo were nowhere in sight, and I was glad. I'd seen him one time today, and that was enough.

Back inside of the apartment, I lit a few candles and popped the DVD inside of the DVD player. After freshening up a bit, I put on a pair of yoga pants and a white tank top. Then I went back in the living room and waited for Mark to call. He called as soon as he got outside and came to the apartment door. Before he knocked, I opened the door and let him in. I was surprised to see that he was carrying a few bags of grocery as he entered.

"I was going to grab some take-out, but I figured that it wouldn't take much time for me to whip up something," he said.

"You're going to cook?" I asked with a surprised look on my face.

"Yes, ma'am. How does chicken fettuccine sound, with fresh vegetables?"

"That sounds so good. Let me show you to the kitchen," I replied, as I walked around the counter.

I watched him wash and prep the chicken while he boiled the water for the noodles. My stomach growled, and I hope that he hadn't heard the ferocious tiger inside of my belly. As he made the sauce from scratch, I paid close attention because I might want to make this meal one day for myself. When everything was ready, we sat at the table and talked. The food was fantastic and tasted better than any restaurant that we could have gone to. I was glad that we didn't go out, this date seemed more intimate.

When we were finished eating, Mark poured a glass of wine for each of us. While we got comfortable on the couch, I grabbed the remote and pressed play. As the previews played, he moved in closer as I sipped wine from my glass. The sun had already set, and the only light that was on in the apartment came from the television. We both relaxed and watched the screen wondering what was going to happen next until a steamy sex scene unfolded in front of us. By this time, I was already on my third glass of wine and was feeling more than a little frisky.

I didn't think my actions through, as I reached over and started to rub his leg. Mark didn't say anything as the people on the screen acted out the sex scene. I had no idea that they had movies like this in the Redbox. Even though I had just taken a huge sip out of my wine glass, my mouth felt dry when I asked in a low whisper, "Do you mind if I kiss you?" He then looked over at me and shook his head no. Our lips connected and the room went silent. I normally would have been shy, but I had drunk a lot of wine. While we both ignored the movie, I felt both of our hearts thumping. I wanted him more than ever, but I didn't know how to tell him that I was ready for him.

We only made out on the soft leather couch like Trevor and I used to do. My lips were officially kissing another man, and it felt incredible. I hope Mark was enjoying this as much as I was. Before I laid back, I seductively pulled him on top of me. Without crushing me with his body weight, he kissed me passionately. My hips rotated in slow motion as my legs opened up for him. I knew that something was about to happen until my phone rang. I wasn't going to answer it, but Mark sat up and excused himself to the bathroom.

When I looked at the screen on my phone, I saw Trevor's name. *"What in the hell did he want?"* I thought before I answered.

"What in the hell is that guy doing in my apartment?" He scolded.

"What?"

"You heard me. You've got five minutes to get him out of there, or I'm coming over," he said as he hung up. Mark came back from the bathroom just as I put my cell phone down. "I should go," he said, as he bent down and gave me one final kiss on the lips. I didn't argue since I knew that Trevor was coming over. I only thanked him for dinner and a good time and let him leave.

Not even two minutes after Mark left, I heard a knock at my door and opened it without asking because I knew who it was.

"What in the hell is up with you? How are you going to tell me to see other people and then you call my phone acting all crazy?"

"You shouldn't have had that guy in our place."

"Well you've got some nerve," I shouted as he walked through the apartment.

"Yeah, I'm still paying the bills here, I can come in here and do whatever I want, whenever I want."

"No, you can't. That wasn't the agreement."

"Well, it's the agreement now. Come here and give me some sweet sugar," he demanded as I resisted his touch.

"Trevor you need to leave. Go back down the walkway to your new chick."

"Damn, it's like that Summer?"

"Yes, that's exactly how it is," I hissed as I opened the door to the apartment.

"So you're just going to kick me out of my apartment?" He asked as he walked towards me and disregarded the open door. I guess a bit of my mother's sassiness jumped into my spirit, and before I knew it, I let him have it.

"I don't know what kind of sick, twisted game you're trying to play with my heart, but I've had just about enough of it. Your name may be on the lease to this apartment, but you don't own me. I don't know who in the hell you think you are. I know that I can do better than you and I don't deserve to be treated like this."

My eyes welled up with tears and my nostrils flared as he and I stood face to face.

"I'll tell you exactly who I am! I'm the one who paid your bony black ass some attention in high school when no one else would even give you a second look. I'm the one who popped your cherry on the handmade quilt that my grandmother made. I'm the one who gave the moving company the go-ahead to move all of this top of the line furniture back in here. I'm the one who doesn't give a good damn about those wedding invitations in there on that shelf, and last, but not least I'm the one who's paying this high ass rent because you can't afford to pay it with your measly paychecks. That's who the hell I am. Now give me a damn kiss," he said as he grabbed my face and stuck his tongue into my mouth.

I jerked my head away from him and pushed him out of the apartment. Before he had a chance to react, I slammed and locked the door in his face. While I stood on the inside, my chest heaved up and down. I never saw Trevor behave this way. This seeing other people thing was his idea, not mine. On my way into the bedroom, I turned off the DVD that Mark and I had been watching and called my mother to tell her that I was coming to Miami. She was beyond excited and mentioned again that she had someone she wanted me to meet. I was going to ask her who this someone was when I heard a beep.

After looking down at the screen of my cell phone, I saw that Mark was calling, and I told my mother that I had to go. She sounded bummed out but perked back up when I promised to call her in the morning. When I clicked back over, Mark told me that he was almost home and called to say how much he enjoyed our date. While he talked, I replayed the events that happened on the sofa in my head and wished that we would have gone all the way.

5

Hauling Ass

That Monday morning, I dressed and made sure that I had all of my things packed before the locksmith came. I hired him to change the locks on the doors. While I rolled my suitcases and carry-on bag outside to my car, he worked quickly. When he finished, he closed the entry door and handed me the key to unlock it. I already knew that the key was going to work because I saw him unlock it right before he called me over. This must've been something that he did when he was finished with a new lock installation. After I successfully unlocked the door, we both walked inside and tried the new key on the patio door, and it worked as well. Then I handed him a check and thanked him while he thanked me for selecting his company to get the job done.

Before I left, I checked to make sure that I had packed everything that I would need in Miami. I noticed that I'd left my sleep mask on the nightstand and grabbed it. After I had tucked it into the back pocket of my shorts, I made sure that all the lights were off and that the windows were locked. I then shut the door to the apartment and locked the newly installed deadbolt from the outside.

I peeked my head around the corner and saw Trevor's car, but he was nowhere in sight, and I was thankful. I didn't want to see him at all today after he let himself into the apartment yesterday. I was taking a shower, and he walked into the bathroom on me. He almost scared me half to death, and he even tried to have sex with me after I got out of the shower. Needless to say, I rejected him, then he got mad and stormed out. This was the reason I got the new locks installed today. I didn't want him thinking that he could just barge into the apartment whenever he wanted to. I didn't care if he was still paying the rent or not.

I wasn't sure if he knew it, but he'd pushed me to the edge, and I could no longer stomach being anywhere near him. I didn't know who this person was he changed into, but I didn't like it at all. As much as I didn't want to admit it, I think that going to Miami is the best thing for me at the moment. I hated to leave the budding relationship that Mark and I were developing, but I had to go. If it were meant to be, he would wait for me until I returned. When I popped up on him at work, he was surprised and greeted me with a warm hug. We chatted a little, and he was all smiles until I told him that I was going to Miami for a few weeks. The look on his face was a bit disheartening, and I gave him a long kiss in the middle of the produce department before I told him goodbye.

When the clock struck eleven, I was on my way to my eye doctor's appointment. I was nervous and excited because I was going to pick up my contacts today. After I had checked in with the receptionist, the doctor called me back to a room and showed me a short video. Then I practiced taking the flexible contact lenses in and out of my eyes. I was having a little trouble, so the doctor washed his hands and removed his lenses a few times until I caught on. I practiced in the mirror in one of the eye exam rooms for another thirty minutes, and I was a professional. The honey colored contacts looked amazing, and I was glad that I decided to step outside of the box and try something new.

With my flight taking off in a little over an hour, I high-tailed it to the airport. After parking, I rolled my bags inside and checked my luggage in. Not too long after that, I was flying the friendly skies. I didn't know what to expect out of this Miami trip, but I hoped that I had a good time; most of all I hoped that Trevor would be back to his normal self when I returned.

When I knocked on the door to my mother's apartment, a little girl answered that looked to be no more than eleven or twelve. She didn't say anything. She only let me in and went back to sit on the mismatched furniture in front of the television. "Hi," I said as I closed the entry door. "Hi," she replied, without taking her eyes off of the television.

"Is my mom here?" I asked as I set my luggage down and sat beside her on the couch.

"No, they went to the fish market I think. They shouldn't be gone long because my dad has a new car that goes real fast."

"Oh really."

"Yes. You're Summer right?" The girl asked.

"Yes, but don't you think you should've established that before you let me in here?"

"No, I know how you look. There are pictures of you all around this apartment. Only you don't have glasses or the wig, or weave. That is a weave isn't it?"

I couldn't believe the audacity of this little heffa," I thought as I stared at her and said, "It's none of your business. What's your name anyway?"

"My name is Imani."

From that moment, Imani stuck to me like glue. She watched me while I started to unpack and offered me an ice pop. I accepted her offer, and thought of Mark's sensitive teeth while selecting a grape popsicle. After consuming the refreshing treat, she helped me unpack the rest of my things. Then we went back to the living room and waited for my mom and her dad to return.

I scrolled through the images on my phone while Imani watched television. I studied the pictures of Trevor and me, and could see the unhappiness in his face. He wasn't smiling on any of the pictures. All he had was this blank expression on his face. I wonder how long he's held in the thought of seeing other people. That's one question that I didn't bother to ask him. When I started deleting the pictures one by one, my eyes grew blurry. As the first set of tears escaped my tear ducts. I heard loud laughing in the hallway outside of the apartment door and quickly wiped my face with the collar of my shirt. I knew it was my mom. I knew her loud laugh if I didn't know anyone else's. I sniffed and wiped my face one more time before I opened the door.

"Mom," I yelled as I wrapped both of my arms around her neck.

"My baby is finally here. Aw, let me look at you," she said as she gave me another hug and added, "Oh Summer, this is my boyfriend, Lester."

"Hi Lester," I said as he looked me up and down.

"No ma'am, I don't want no dry ass hi, I want one of those hugs like you gave your mother," he said in a raspy voice.

I hoped he wasn't serious because I wasn't going to hug him. I didn't even know him, what made him think that I was going to give him a hug.

"Lester, leave her alone and take that seafood into the kitchen," my mother said.

"I was just messing with the little lady," he admitted while he handed Imani a lollipop from his pocket.

"Thanks, Dad," she happily said.

While Imani unwrapped her treat, my mom gave me another hug and said, "I hope you're hungry. We just bought a lot of food."

"I could eat," I answered.

Just then, Lester called her in the kitchen, and she disappeared around the corner. With the ocean a few blocks away, I asked Imani if she wanted to go for a walk and she hopped off of the couch.

"Hey Mom, how long before the food is ready?" I shouted.

"We still have to scale the fish and shell the shrimp, so it will be about an hour. You know it doesn't take me long to cook," she responded.

"Well, if it's okay with Lester, I'd like to take Imani for a walk to the ocean real quick."

"That's fine," Lester said as he peeked his head from around the corner.

After receiving the confirmation from Lester, Imani and I left the apartment. As we walked, things started to seem familiar to me all over again.

"That's where the lady sells frozen Kool-Aid and candy to the neighborhood kids and some adults," Imani said as she looked in the direction of the house.

The place looked unkept, and I doubted if I would want to eat or drink anything that came from there. I kept my comment to myself as we continued to walk. Next, we passed by a house with tall black metal fencing wrapped around its perimeter. Just as I was about to ask why they had such a high fence, two overgrown Doberman Pinschers ran from the back of the house.

While the dogs carried on and barked in a manner that was very threatening, we both ignored them and kept walking. With only one house left to pass before we crossed the street, I remembered the girl that I used to visit at this house. We used to be good friends back in middle school, but I couldn't remember her name to save my life. As I searched my memory, I think that I recalled staying the night at this house before. Before we crossed the street, I looked back and gave the house a long stare, but it was useless. I didn't remember my friend's name.

The ocean was in plain view, and it never looked so good to me. I couldn't wait to lay out in the sun and play in the water. As we got closer to the shore Imani and I took our flip flops off. Since we both were wearing shorts, we welcomed the warm crystal clear water without hesitation. I was knee deep in the salt water and ready to take a swim until I remembered the food mom was cooking back at the apartment. We frolicked in the water a little more before I said, "We better start walking back. The food is probably ready." "Okay," she replied as we roamed slowly towards the shore.

I could tell that she didn't want to leave the ocean. I didn't want to leave either, but I was hungry. I hadn't eaten any of my mom's cooking in a long time, and my mouth started to water just thinking about the meal that was waiting for us. My stomach growled as we approached the house that looked very familiar to me. While I tried to remember my friend's name again, a voice yelled from the shaded front porch, "Summer is that you?" "Yes, it's me," I answered as I stopped walking and looked at the lady.

Sitting on the porch in an orange lounge chair was a very familiar face. As she got up and walked towards the white picket fence, I remembered her name. It was Johaly, the only girl that my mother allowed to spend the night at our apartment. My long lost best friend was right here in front of me, and I could not believe it. This didn't seem real at all, and she still looked the same. I've heard of the saying *"Black don't crack"* and in her case, this was one hundred percent accurate.

I instantly remembered her name and shouted, "Oh my God Johaly, is that you?"

"Yes, it's me," she yelled as she tore down the walkway and unlatched the fence. She hugged me tightly, and I hugged her back. Meanwhile, Imani looked at us like we both were crazy.

"Is this your daughter?" She asked as she looked down at Imani.

"Oh no. Imani is a friend of the family."

"No, I'm not, I'm your sister," Imani blurted.

I looked at her like she was crazy.

"Imani, be quiet while Johaly and I talk," I snapped.

She did as I said and folded her arms. I could tell that she was angry because she stomped on ants while Johaly and I continued with our conversation.

"So do you live here in Miami?" She asked as she leaned against the fence.

"No, I'm visiting my mom for the summer, she lives a few blocks away from here."

"Does she still live in that same apartment?"

"Yep."

"If I would have known that I could have stopped by there and got your phone number. I've been thinking about you like crazy."

"Is that your house?" I asked as I pointed to the two story house behind her.

"No. I wish it were. I'm here for the summer too. I'm house sitting for my aunt and uncle. When they asked if I could watch their place, I didn't hesitate because it's so close to the ocean. Don't you remember them? You stayed a few nights here with me before when we were in middle school."

I thought, and I vaguely remembered that her aunt was short and plump, and her uncle was the total opposite.

"Yeah, I remember them," I said with a giggle before I added, "That's great. Are you married? Do you have any kids?"

"Child, no. I'm not trying to get murdered. I meant married."

After a few more minutes of small talk, I told Johaly that Imani and I had to go. We exchanged numbers and left to go back to the apartment. As we walked down the hall that led to mom's apartment in silence, I blurted, "What was up with you back there Imani? Why did you lie? You know that you're not my sister. Your dad dates my mom and that's it."

"My dad and your mom got married. I am your sister," she said with an attitude.

My mind had officially been blown. Had my mom gotten married and didn't tell me?

"You're a lying little cunt," I said as I entered my mother's apartment.

Imani tried to run into the kitchen before I could get there, but I beat her. While I called for my mom, she called for her dad.

"Dad, tell Summer that I'm her sister."

"Mom, please tell me that you didn't get married without telling me," I said as I looked into her eyes.

After Imani and I had questioned our parents in unison, there was a brief moment of silence. The look on my mother's face told me what I wanted to know without her saying a word.

"Summer, don't be mad. I wanted to tell you, but..."

"But nothing Mom, how could you?"

"We'll be right back Lester and Imani. You two can start eating if you want to," Mom said.

"No, that's okay baby, we'll wait until you and Summer get back," Lester said.

My mom took me by the hand and walked towards my old bedroom.

"Summer calm down. I mentioned several times that I wanted to tell you about someone special, but you always managed to get off of the phone before I could say anything about Lester. I still didn't want you to find out this way. We were going to share the news about the marriage over dinner this evening. I was going to tell you."

I thought back to the times when Mom had mentioned someone special in our phone conversations, and I did indeed brush her off. If I had listened, I wouldn't have gotten surprised like this today. I was dead wrong for being upset, and I apologized.

"I'm sorry, Mom. I am happy for you and Lester. Congratulations," I said as I gave her a hug. On the way back to the kitchen, I wanted to cry. How on earth did my mom get married before I did? I wasn't expecting this and had to admit that I was a little jealous.

After I had sat down beside my new sister, I apologized for calling her a cunt and even shot a smile at my handsome stepdad. I tried my best not to think about what Trevor was doing with his pecan tan gal pal, but I couldn't. The thought of him spending time with someone else almost made me sick to my stomach. To get my mind off of Trevor, I started asking Lester all kinds of questions, and he opened up like a book in front of me. I learned that he owned a roofing company and that Imani was his only child.

After our seafood dinner, I showered the salty sea water down the drain and went into my room for some privacy. Imani wanted to come in with me, but I told her no. After I shut and locked the door, I sat on the edge of the bed and thought about calling Trevor. I guess he was thinking about me too because my phone rang and his name lit up on the screen. I quickly answered, and he apologized for coming into the apartment unannounced yesterday. I accepted his apology after he swore that he'd never do anything like that again.

"So where have you been? I haven't seen your car all day," he admitted.

"Trevor, I'm in Miami," I confessed.

"That's great. I know that your mother was happy to see you. You are at your mother's right?"

"Yes, Trevor. I'm at my mom's. I'll be here for a month or so."

"Oh, well. I just wanted to say I'm sorry, and I hope you have a good time."

"Thanks, I appreciate your sincere apology. What are you doing?"

"We're about to check out this new club, I was in the middle of getting ready, and I couldn't stop thinking about you."

I didn't care to know who we were, so I didn't ask. I assumed that he and his best bud were going to a strip club. I was a little bitter about this, but I didn't show my jealousy. Besides, there wasn't a damn thing I could do about it.

Even though Trevor was getting ready, he asked me about the flight and my mom. When I told him that she got married, he asked dozens of questions. He couldn't believe that she'd jumped the broom either. After he had asked me about mom, he asked me about Lester. Then I told him that I had a stepsister too.

"Damn, you haven't even been there twenty-four hours, and you gained a new daddy and a sister. That's a bit much to take in," he said.

"Yes, it is. I'm still shocked, to tell you the truth."

"Well, what are your plans for the evening?" He asked.

"I just got out of the shower. I'll probably invite my new sister in my room and let her take control of the television. She's probably waiting at the door now."

"Promise me that you'll try to have fun while you're in Miami, and keep in touch with me so I know what's going on with you."

"I promise, but I'm not going to have any fun tonight," I replied as a yawn escaped my mouth.

I still couldn't believe that he wanted me to go out and meet other men. This whole idea seemed a little insane to me, but if that's what he wanted me to do, I was going to do it. I just hoped that Trevor would get this out of his system and let me mail out those wedding invitations when I got back to Texas. Even though he and I were separated, I still felt attached to him. Before I called Imani into my room, I unlocked the door. She ran in and jumped on my full-size bed. Then without asking she got under the covers and said, "I hope you don't snore."

———•━•●•━•———

The next morning I woke up to a rocking sound followed by low moans. It only took me a second to realize that Mom and Lester were knocking boots. As much as I tried not to listen, I couldn't help it because my room shared a wall with my mother's. I wanted to put the pillow over my head, but I was afraid to move. I didn't want to wake Imani. God knows she didn't need to hear this nastiness. I shut my eyes and begged the sandman to come back and sprinkle me with his sleeping dust, but he didn't. I was forced to listen to my mom and new stepdad make love. When the rocking sound got faster, the moans grew a little louder, and I wasn't sure if mom was making the noise or if it was Lester.

At that moment, I prayed that God would take my sense of hearing away. Not permanently, just temporarily. That way I wouldn't hear them going at it like two rabbits. Lester had to be popping Viagra or something because the rocking sound didn't stop until almost an hour later. When they were done, I heard muffled talking and the sound of the shower starting.

While Imani slept with one of her legs hanging off of the bed, I debated on getting up. When I heard the television in the living room come on, I made my move and put on my robe. As soon as I opened my bedroom door, Lester said, "Good morning Summer." "Good morning," I replied and walked to the bathroom across the hallway. After washing my face and brushing my teeth, I came out and darted back into my room. When I returned, Imani was up.

"I'm hungry," she said, as she stretched.

"Is there any cereal in the kitchen?"

"There is, but there isn't any milk," she answered.

"How far is the corner store from here?" I asked as I stepped inside of the small walk-in closet and slipped on a pair of shorts.

"Not far. Do you want me to go with you?"

"Yes. You can go, but you have to wash your face and brush your teeth first."

The store was four blocks away. I thought that it was hot in Texas, I forgot about the humidity here in Miami. It was so thick that I felt as if it would take my breath away. When we walked into the store that was only a few degrees cooler than it was outside, I had a trail of sweat dripping down my back. I needed to find some cold air fast because I feared that I was going to faint. While I pretended to look in the beer cooler, I enjoyed the cold blast of air that poured out. The man behind the counter at the store smiled at me as I stood with the door wide open.

When my internal temperature had dropped, I walked over to the milk cooler. Imani had already grabbed a jug, but after I had checked the expiration date on it, I returned it to the cooler and searched for another one.

"Is there anything I can help you with?" The guy asked from behind the counter.

"Um, no. I think I found what we needed," I replied as I grabbed another jug of milk and asked Imani if she wanted anything else while we were at the store.

"I'd like a drink, some chips, a few pieces of bubble gum, and some penny candy."

"Get whatever you want and put it on the counter."

Imani didn't hold back and got all the candy that her heart desired. While I waited for her by the counter, the voice in my head told me to buy some condoms and a few scratch-off lottery tickets. I always followed my gut instincts and purchased the condoms and lottery tickets while Imani shopped. After I had paid for the condoms, I stuffed the box inside of my purse so Imani wouldn't see them. While I waited for her, I scratched the lottery tickets with a dime. The first three tickets were a total waste of my hard earned money, but the fourth one was a winner.

"I can't believe it, I won. I won three hundred dollars," I yelled as I waved the ticket in the air.

"Congratulations, pretty lady. Would you like your payout in small bills or big bills?" The guy said from behind the counter.

"Um, big bills. I guess."

"Your wish is my command," he said as he scanned the ticket and handed me my winnings.

After Imani had brought her things to the counter, I paid, and we left the store. On the way home, she drank a carton of Jungle Juice and ate chips, while I carried everything else. When we reached the apartment, I didn't tell mom about my lottery win. I only put the milk in the refrigerator and ate the pancakes and bacon that she'd made for breakfast.

With our bellies full and the sun shining brightly outside, Imani and I decided to go back to the beach today. Before we put on our bathing suits, I called Johaly and asked her if she wanted to go with us. She agreed but told me that there was a pool in her aunt and uncle's backyard. It seemed that today was getting better and better. As we prepared to leave with a beach bag full of towels, sunblock, and the penny candy she'd gotten from the store earlier. I told Lester and my mother that we would be back later. When they both nodded and smiled, a part of me wondered if the two of them were going to get it on again before he went to work.

We walked in silence as we approached the yard of the dilapidated neighborhood treat house. It was full of children of all ages. They were holding small Styrofoam cups. Some of them waved at Imani as they tilted their cups up to the sky and sipped on the sweet liquid. I wanted a Kool-Aid slush but resisted the urge to purchase one when I saw the owner of the house come outside in a stained housecoat with a poodle on a leash. As I thought about how the refreshing drink would make my dry throat feel, we passed by the house with the mean dogs, and approached a white picket fence.

Johaly was waiting for us on the front porch of her aunt and uncle's place. When she saw us, she walked to the fence and waited for us. Then without saying a word, she joined us, and we all walked to the beach. There were a lot of people here already, and we had a hard time finding a good spot to set our umbrella up. Johaly located a small patch of sand near some cute guys in no time. I was a little uncomfortable around them, but she interacted with them like she'd known them her entire life.

After I had overheard that their names were Manny and Dante', I thought of how I'd never met anyone named Manny. Maybe his name was short for Emmanuel or something. While I thought about the name, I wondered if the guys were Cuban or Dominican. They could have been black like me for all I knew, but they did have a bit of an accent. I watched both of the fellows closely as Johaly dug into her beach bag and retrieved a bottle of suntan lotion. "Would you like for me to help put that on your back?" Dante' asked with a huge crocodile smile. "Yeah, that would be great," she said as she handed him the bottle.

Before she turned over on her stomach, she untied the strings on her bikini top. "I can't stand tan lines," she stated as she got comfortable. Dante' then knelt down and squeezed some lotion into his hands. After he had rubbed it between his palms, he caressed her shoulders. Johaly's face looked like she was in heaven as his hands moved lower. Seeing her get slathered down with suntan lotion reminded me that I hadn't put on any sunblock yet. Unlike Johaly, I didn't want or need a tan, so I reached in my bag for my sun block. As I looked up, Manny was eyeballing me.

I automatically knew what he thought when he saw my sun block. When he opened his mouth and said, "You need help with that?"

I only smiled and shook my head yes. "My name is Summer."

"Nice to meet you. My name is Manny."

"It's nice to meet you too."

Instead of laying on my stomach, I sat in Indian style as Manny squirted sunblock between his palms. When he began to rub the sunblock on my back and shoulders, I snuck a peek at Dante'. He was still applying lotion to Johaly's lower back and had an erection. I almost burst out laughing when I noticed it. The front of his orange swimming trunks resembled one of those orange safety cones. I didn't know if Johaly knew it or not, but she was turning him on.

I turned my attention back to Manny, as he continued to rub my back, it almost felt like he was giving me a massage. Since seeing Dante's erection, I had sex on my brain. I tried not to stare at Manny, but I couldn't keep my eyes off of him and his six pack. I thought Trevor looked good without his shirt on, but this guy clearly had him beat. After he had completed the task, he stood up and handed me the bottle of sunblock. I thanked him, and he only replied with a smile that made me forget all about Trevor. Manny was super handsome. He was just as dark as I was and he had brown eyes that matched his skin. I wanted to ask him if he was wearing contacts, but I was too shy.

The feeling that I felt was indescribable. I had the hots for this muscular man, and I'd only met him fifteen minutes ago. How could that be possible? Not long after Manny applied my sunblock, I got up to frolic with Imani in the water. While she splashed water on me, I chased her playfully. In between playing with her, I watched Johaly and the two guys interacting. I wondered what they were saying while I was over here. Was Manny asking her questions about me? I hoped that she got their phone numbers as I walked down the beach with Imani.

The further we strolled the more shirtless guys I saw. I feared that my eyes would bulge out of my head as I stared at their biceps and gorgeous faces. Where on earth did all of these good looking men come from? They sure weren't here when I was in high school, well they could have been; I was just too wrapped up in Trevor to realize it. While Imani and I walked the shore, I enjoyed all the eye candy. I now understood why Trevor suggested that we take a break with our relationship. I'd never got a chance to have fun, date, or be single either. Just from looking at all of these beautiful people, I knew that it was going to be one hot summer.

6

Hot and Bothered

I didn't know what I was going to wear to the bar tonight. Johaly and I wore the same size, so I tried on some of her things.

"Girl you got a cute shape. I wish I had hips like that."

"These saddle bags run in our family and no matter how much I exercise they never go away."

"You are stacked, you shouldn't be at the gym doing a thing," Johaly said, as she handed me a mini skirt from out of her suitcase.

"This is cute, but I've never worn anything this short before, I'm not sure about this."

"Just put the skirt on and see how it looks."

I did as she said, and she was right. I looked good in this skirt.

"We need to go to the mall so that I can purchase a few of these. Do you think we can go?"

"Why wouldn't we be able to go? I've got the keys to my aunt's drop top Mercedes and the tank is full of gas."

Johaly and I smiled as we looked at each other and grabbed our purses. When we got in the car, she started the engine, pushed a button, and the convertible top disappeared. We cruised through the city with the hot sun beaming down on us. I wished that she would have put the top up, but I didn't say anything. If I was going to be riding shotgun in a convertible all summer, I needed to add shades and a sun hat to my shopping list today.

Before we went to the mall, we stopped by Target. After Johaly had picked up the items she needed for the house, we browsed through the ladies clothing. When she came across a rack of shorts that were on sale, she called for me to come over.

When I saw how short the shorts were on the hanger, I couldn't bring myself to put them in my shopping basket. But when Johaly left to try on a pair in the dressing room, I figured that I'd try on a pair too. After sliding on the shorts, my mouth flew open. I couldn't believe that my legs looked so good, and I called her to look. "I knew that they would look good on you," she said as she peeked through the dressing room door at me. I ended up purchasing two pairs of shorts, five tank tops, three bikinis, two straw hats, and a pair of shades.

I couldn't wait to see what the mall had in store for us. I tried to remember that I needed to stick to my budget, just in case Trevor and I didn't work out. I didn't want to go crazy and spend all of my money on my second day here in Miami. The lottery money was a blessing, but three hundred dollars couldn't even pay one fourth of my rent. As I tried to forget about my worries back at home in Texas, I continued to shop as I paid close attention to the price tags.

Considering that I'd already spent almost one hundred and fifty dollars in Target, I only picked up a few more items from the mall. When we left, the sun had set, and there was no need for shades or a straw hat. I let the wind blow through my hair as I enjoyed the ride.

Back at the beach house Johaly and I showered and got dressed. I wore a short yellow body dress and a pair of wedge sandals. I had to admit, I looked good and never thought in a million years that I'd be going to a club with my middle school bestie. I was so glad that we'd found each other after all these years. As I put in my honey colored contacts, Johaly stopped dead in her tracks. "Girl, those are pretty. They look great with your complexion. I think you need a little eye makeup to make your eyes pop. Sit here; I think that this eyeshadow will look good." I was a little hesitant to sit at her makeup area because she had a lot of makeup spread out on the bathroom counter.

Secretly, my new contacts were enough for me, but I let her fix my face up without saying a word. I'd never used any cosmetics before and was blown away by her work. When I looked in the mirror for the very first time wearing the eyeshadow, eyeliner, and mascara. I was in shock. I looked totally different and wanted to spend the last of my lottery winnings on makeup.

"This is amazing. I can't believe that I look like this."

"Why are you shocked? You're beautiful, Summer. This eye makeup only brings out your eyes."

"Thanks, I bet if Trevor were to see me tonight he wouldn't want to date other people."

"Right. Oh, you never finished telling me about that whole crazy situation," she said.

"I'll tell you, but right now let's meet up with these guys."

We got to the bar in no time and saw the guys from the beach as soon as we walked in. All eyes were on us as we entered the sophisticated setup. When she said that we were going to a bar, I suspected a hole in the wall with a jukebox in the corner and drunken men with beer bellies hanging over their belt buckles. This wasn't the case.

The walls were painted a teal color that fell somewhere between the color turquoise and sky blue on the color wheel. The floors were a shiny glazed concrete, and there was chrome blinged-out chandeliers hanging from the ceiling. The bar had a marble countertop that stretched from one end of the place to the other. There seemed to be twenty top of the line barstools lined up at an angle in front of the bar, and three bartenders were busy mixing drinks for the party goers as I continued to take it all in.

While I was amazed at the seamless mirror wall behind the bar, the liquor selection caught my eye. As we walked past the four expensive pool tables, I saw that there was a hookah lounge on the other side of the bar, as well as a dance floor, and a few old school video game machines near the restrooms. I'd never seen a bar like this. To me, this place shouldn't have been called a bar at all. This was a club, no doubt about it.

Manny and Dante' waved us over to the bar, and we walked over. They both wore button down short sleeved polo shirts, cargo shorts, and the latest Jordan sneakers. I only knew about these because my students talked about the popular shoes so much. I wondered why their outfits were the same except for different colors until I looked closely at them. They were twins. I didn't see it earlier, but now I could. Dante' had braids and Manny had a fresh fade. They both had neat beards. Only Manny had a little more facial hair than his brother.

In no time, Manny and I got familiar with each other and gulped down drinks like they were free. Just when I'd made my mind up that I wasn't going to drink anything else tonight, he offered to buy me another. I couldn't resist and accepted his offer. As I watched Johaly and Dante' play pool, I started sipping on my fourth alcoholic beverage. The fruity drink tasted like a blend of life savers, pineapple juice, and top shelf liquor. While I continued to drink, I wondered how Manny's lips tasted.

"Do you want to play one of those video games over there?" He pointed. "Yeah, I'm sure that'll be fun," I replied as he settled our debt with the bartender. When I stood up, all the liquor that I had drank in the two hour time span had just made its way to my cooch. I felt hotter than hot as we walked towards the video games in the dimly lit corner.

Since I lost the first two games of Pac-Man, Manny moved in close and wrapped his arms and hands around mine. With his pelvis pressing up against my posterior, I grew more and more aroused. I shut my eyes and breathed in his scent while his hands were on top of mine maneuvering the joysticks. I knew that he felt it when I moved my body closer to him because his member hardened instantly. I felt the lump in his cargo shorts hardening more and more by the second. When he placed a kiss on my neck, my flesh grew weak, and I couldn't take it. I took him by the hand and led him outside.

"I want you right now," I said, as I pulled him into the alley.

"Are you serious?"

"Hell yes. I wanted you ever since I saw you this morning."

After I had made my confession, I pressed Manny up against the building and let my hands roam all over his body. When our lips met, it was over. My hands greedily unbuckled his cargo shorts and reached inside of his boxers. I was taken by surprise because Manny was much larger than Trevor. I grew more excited by the second as I hiked my skirt up and jumped on him.

I held onto him tightly, with my arms wrapped around his neck. We exchanged sloppy kisses as he reached down and pulled my panties to the side. He pierced me with his erection, and it felt different. It was a good different, though. Now that he was already inside of me, I wanted to see his blessing. I wished I would have asked before we started having sex, but it was too late now. I smelled the liquor on his breath as he sucked on my neck. With his hands palming my behind, I moaned and couldn't think of anywhere else that I'd rather be at this moment. "I can't take too much more of this. You've got to get down," he said. "Alright," I agreed as he withdrew himself from my warm, juicy opening.

That's when I saw it, Manny's penis was sticking straight out. Considering that it was dim in the alley, I still couldn't believe my eyes as I gawked at it. I felt the urge to fall on my knees and pleasure him, but before I could insist, he said, "Bend over and put your hands on the wall." I followed his instructions and he slipped into my wetness once again. He delivered deep thrusts as I arched my back and took all that he had to offer. Then, without any warning, he pulled away from me and his love juice squirted onto the brick wall that I was leaning against. While he made all kinds of weird noises and yanked at his penis, I pulled my wet panties off and tucked them into my bra.

After I had pulled my dress down, I looked around to see if anyone had seen what just happened in the alley. I didn't see anyone, and I only heard the music pumping from the other side of the wall of the building. While Manny fixed himself back up, I waited patiently without saying anything. "You ready to go back inside now?" He asked as he reached for my hand. "Yeah, let's go back inside. I'd like to buy you a drink," I replied with a villainous laugh.

Back in the bar, I headed to the bathroom and tossed my soaked undies in the garbage can. Then I freshened up at the sink and hoped that no one walked inside to see me taking a whore's bath. I dried my cooch off with some napkins and stood under the air blow dryer for a second and I was ready to go back to the bar with Manny. When I walked back out, I saw that Johaly and Dante' were still playing pool. I caught her eye as she waited for her turn and she gave me a thumbs up. I guess that meant that she was winning because she had a huge smile on her face.

I returned the smile and headed back to Manny. Now that he'd blown my back out, I was more attracted to him. I bought him a drink like I said I would, and talked with him until the bar was about to close. I was sad to know that Manny and Dante' were only vacationing and didn't live here in Miami. They were only two days into their seven-day vacation and planned to come and hang out with us again before they left. Before Johaly and I pulled away in the Mercedes, Manny and I exchanged numbers. Then we shared a long hug, and he kissed me on the lips.

The ride home was like an amusement park ride, and I felt car sick. I didn't know if my motion sickness was from Johaly's drunk driving or if I'd drank too much. Whatever the case, I had to tell her what happened so I fought the urge to puke and started talking.

"Tonight was crazy," I blurted.

"Tell me about it. I won six rounds of pool."

"Girl, Dante' let you win. Even I saw the game he was running on you," I informed her with a giggle.

"Oh, hush up. I know how to play pool. Hey, where did you and Manny sneak off to? Y'all were gone for a good twenty minutes or so. I was about to look for you."

"I'm a big girl, Johaly. I appreciate your concern and all, but I can handle myself."

"Okay, Miss. Thang. I hear you. Well, where in the hell did you go?"

I left her hanging with a moment of silence before she yelled, "Come on Summer. Tell me!"

I was done telling her the details about Manny and me in the alley, as she pulled up in front of my mother's apartment building.

"Maybe I can get me some good loving before they leave. Do you think that Dante' is packing like his brother?" She asked.

"I think he may be because he had a very noticeable erection whenever he was applying that suntan lotion on your back at the beach this morning."

"He did?" Johaly squealed.

"Yes, he sure did."

The next day we went to the beach without Imani. She was mad that I left her at home, but she would have to get over it because Johaly and I were on the prowl. We decided that we would have a small get together at her aunt's beach house. We printed a few flyers and made sure that we put BYOB (bring your own beer) in big bold letters at the top. I was sure that lots of people would come because of the pool and free food. The two of us would have never been able to pull this off without two of Johaly's friends. One needed money for her light bill and sold some of her food stamps to us dirt cheap, and the other worked at a fried chicken joint and offered us a few free boxes of chicken. We were going to pick up everything after we left the beach.

I frolicked around in a lime green bikini and handed out a few flyers to a group of cute girls. Next, I gave a flyer to a guy who reminded me of Mark. That reminded me, I hadn't talked to him and needed to call him. After passing out a few more flyers, I looked for the hot pink umbrella that Johaly and I set up earlier.

When I spotted it, I headed in that direction and collapsed on my rented beach chair. I didn't see Johaly anywhere in sight as I looked around. She must've been passing out flyers further down the beach. After taking a sip from my water bottle, I reached into my bag for my cell phone. To my surprise, I had a missed call from Mark. *"I guess the two of us were thinking about each other,"* I thought to myself as I called him back.

The phone rang twice, and he answered in a cheerful tone.

"Hey, there. I was calling to see how everything was going in beautiful Miami."

"It's so good to hear your voice. Things are going great. I'm enjoying myself. How are things back in Dallas?"

"Things in Dallas are great, I had the interview at the police station yesterday, and I got the job."

"That's wonderful. So, when is your last day at the grocery store?"

"I'm still going to work here part-time. I like it because it keeps my mind off of things that happened over in Afghanistan. Plus, it's not like I have a wife or kids to keep me busy at home."

"Oh, I understand," I added.

"Not, unless you want to get married as soon as you get back to Dallas," he chuckled.

"You are a mess."

"You know that I'm only kidding, but there is something that I need to ask you when you get back home."

"Why can't you ask me now?" I questioned.

"Because I want to ask this question face to face and because my break is over."

"Whatever you say, Mark. I'll talk to you later," I blurted before we ended the call.

"What in the world could he want to ask me?" I thought as I saw Johaly walking in my direction. As she flopped down in the chair beside me, she said, "All I could get is six people to promise that they would come tonight. How many people did you get to come?"

"Umm, let me see. A group of five girls, a group of six guys, and one guy that was sitting by himself," I replied.

"Well, that's enough, if all of them come that would give us a backyard full of people. Are you ready to go to the grocery store so we can prepare for this shindig?"

"Yep, let's do this," I replied as I got up and pulled the umbrella from the mound of sand it was resting in.

When we got back to the beach house, Johaly and I both put on a pair of tiny shorts and headed to the grocery store. As we backed out of the driveway, I called my mother's apartment. Imani answered the phone, and I was glad because I was calling for her. "If you want to ride with us to the grocery store, be outside in five minutes and bring a pair of shades." "Okay, I'm on my way out the door now," she replied before she hung up. She was outside when we pulled up just like she said she would be.

"It's about time you came back and got me. It's boring without you here," she mouthed as she settled in the snug back seat.

"You know, it's not too late to leave your behind here," I hissed as she waved toward the window of my mother's apartment.

"Who are you waving at?" Johaly and I asked in unison.

"My daddy. He said that he was going to watch me out of that window until you picked me up."

"Oh, well. I guess I'll wave too," I said while I waved my hand wildly in the direction of the window.

At the grocery store, we picked up buns, hot dogs, pre-made hamburger patties, spicy sausages, potato salad, chips, baked beans, and a few cases of bottled water. I had no clue how we were going to pile all of this stuff into the back seat and trunk of that tiny sports car but it all fit. Johaly almost forgot about picking up the fried chicken until I reminded her. When we turned into the parking lot, we pulled around to the very back of the restaurant. The only thing that was back here were overgrown bushes, a dumpster, and a few stray cats.

After Johaly had made a quick phone call, a guy ran out the back door of the restaurant. He slung a huge bag of chicken to her and waved quickly before running back to the door he had just came out of. "Thanks. I owe you one," she said as she passed me the bag. I set it on my lap, and my thighs felt like they were on fire. The chicken was hotter than I thought it would be and I ended up sitting the bag on the floor by my feet. We had one more stop to make, and that was the store that I'd won the lottery money from. We not only needed gas for the car, but we needed a few jumbo bags of ice too.

Johaly handed me a fifty dollar bill and told me to pay for the gas and four bags of ice. I did as she said and walked inside of the store. When the guy behind the counter saw me in the bikini top and short shorts, his eyes stretched wide. "Hey pretty lady, did you come to press your luck again today?" I laughed and replied, "Not today, I'm only getting gas and four bags of jumbo ice." "Alright," he said as he rang me up.

When he handed me the change from the fifty dollars, I decided that I would press my luck and purchased three more lottery tickets. "Good luck, the ice is on the corner of the store," he said as I walked out of the door. I stuffed the tickets in my back pocket and headed to get the ice. Johaly had just got in the car when I handed Imani the bags of ice. "This is cold," she whined. "Well, there's nowhere else to put it," I said, as I opened my door and sat down by the bag of hot chicken.

As we drove, I pulled the tickets out of my pocket and scratched them with a dime that was in the cup holder. I wasn't so lucky this time. I only won five dollars. When Johaly asked me if we were going to drop Imani off at my mom's apartment, I told her yes. Then we figured that keeping her around would be beneficial to us and called to tell Lester that I would keep her with me.

While Johaly got the food ready, Imani made a sign to hang on the entry gate. The sign read, "Pool party around back." I was in the middle of setting up the boom box and finding some good music when the guy that reminded me of Mark arrived, but he wasn't by himself. There was a beautiful tattooed brown skin girl with him. I remembered his face, but couldn't remember his name, and I was glad when he stuck out his hand and introduced himself. "I'm Leo, and this is my sister Shay," he said. "It's nice to meet the both of you. The party isn't due to start for another hour; you can make yourself comfortable by the pool if you'd like," I said as I continued to mess with the boom box. "I can help you with that," Shay softly spoke as she shot me a smile.

After learning that Shay was a deejay and that she had all sorts of speakers and fancy equipment in her van, I accepted her invitation and let her deal with all the music stuff. While she and Leo, made several trips back and forth to her van, I sat up a few tables for the food. Imani brought the coolers from out the house and poured the bags of ice inside of them. While she positioned the bottles on the ice, I ran upstairs to shower and change into another bikini. This particular bikini was all white with fringe around the bikini top and the bikini bottom front.

When I came back downstairs, Leo had the grill smoking, and a few people had arrived. I didn't know why I hadn't thought about inviting Manny and Dante' until the last minute, but I did. After mentioning it to Johaly. She called Dante' since I was busy picking out music with Shay. I overheard her as she talked to him.

"That's okay. We'll see you guys before you leave. Talk to you later," she said before she hung up.

"They can't come. They already have plans."

"That's okay. We don't need them to have a good time" I said, as I thought about how I wanted another piece of Manny.

"You're right; we can mingle with the guys that come tonight."

7
I Kissed a Girl

Thanks to Leo, Shay, and Imani our party started on time. Imani ended up staying at the party because I didn't want to walk her back home. We gave her strict instructions to lock the door and stay inside of Johaly's room because there were so many strangers around. She had a television, phone, food, and even a bathroom. There was no excuse for her to come out of that room. Depending on what time this party ended, Imani and I both may end up staying the night here.

The music pumped, and people continued to pour in. "I don't remember inviting all these people," Johaly said as two more groups of guys walked in. "As long as there is an equal number of guys to girls we should be good," I said. "Yeah, you're right. I'm going to go inside and get that other jumbo pack of hot dogs." When she went inside, I counted twenty-six people partying in the backyard. Eight people were in the pool, and the rest were mingling around the pool and the food table.

While people ate, drank, and splashed in the pool, I hung out with Shay most of the evening. She showed me how to mix music and let me pick the songs she would play next. I liked her; she was pretty cool. I would have to remember to get her number before she left because I wanted to hang out with the two of them again. They'd helped us out a great deal, and I was glad that I had invited Leo.

I didn't drink a lot at the party considering that everyone brought more than enough alcoholic beverages. I tried to stay sober because I drank a lot the night before with Manny at the bar. While everyone had a blast, I thought about what Manny and I did on the side of the building last night. I still couldn't believe that I had sex with a stranger in an alley. That was totally unlike me, and I was ashamed of myself. I hope that Manny didn't think I was a whore. I'm sure that he knew it was a heat of the moment thing. To be honest, I wished that he was here now. I felt a little alone, even though I was surrounded by people.

When Shay slowed the music down, my thoughts drifted from Manny to Trevor. All of these slow songs reminded me of him. Now I felt sad and wished for a wedding next spring. I was an emotional mess on the inside and wanted to do nothing more than lay down and cry my eyes out. After Shay had announced that she was about to play the last song for the night, I watched a few guys get their mack on before they grabbed their things and prepared to leave. A few of them received phone numbers and even hugs from some ladies. Other guys only received cold shoulders and attitudes. Some guys deserved to get cold shoulders because of the lame pick-up lines they used. I heard one guy say, "I lost my number, can I have yours?" I laughed to myself as the young lady that he was talking to ignored him.

When the only sound that resembled music was crickets chirping, the party came to an end. Before everyone had left, Johaly and I knew that we had a mess on our hands. She insisted that we clean up the mess tomorrow, but Shay and Leo suggested that they could help us tonight. We both agreed to this and started cleaning. Shay and I picked up all the red plastic cups and beer cans while Leo and Johaly took what was left of the food back into the house. When the two of them came back out to join us, Shay and I were sweeping cigarette butts and cigar fillings from the patio.

After we finished cleaning up. We tied the garbage bags up and took them to the green bins on the side of the street. When we returned to the backyard, Leo and Johaly were straightening up the chairs around the pool. The backyard was back to normal. Now the only thing we had to do was put away Shay's deejay equipment. When everything was packed up, Leo rolled a case out to the van and came back to see us all sitting down. "I didn't think that would take that long," Johaly said as she walked towards a teal colored stucco building near the back of the property. "Me either," Shay agreed.

After Johaly had flipped a light switch on the side of the building, a soft glow illuminated a patch of grass near the sidewalk. We all looked in her direction when she said, "Let's have a few more drinks in the pool house." "Pool house?" I said as I stood up. I saw the small building in the corner of the backyard near the fence, but I never thought that it could have been a pool house. I thought that it was a garage. We all agreed to join her for more drinks, but I went in the house to check on Imani first. She was asleep with the television blasting and had no idea that I'd turned it off. After I had covered her up with a thin blanket that was at the foot of the bed, I locked the room door and used the bathroom in the hallway.

When I returned, Johaly had unlocked the pool house, and they were waiting for me inside. Since Johaly was sitting beside Leo, I sat beside Shay. I looked around the tiny room that resembled a studio apartment and saw that there was a bathroom, kitchen, television, couch, and a love seat.

Everything was decorated nicely. I knew that Johaly's aunt and uncle had to be loaded. The pool house was small, but all the furnishings, tile, and appliances were top of the line. While I checked things out, Johaly broke out a couple of shot glasses and a deck of UNO cards. We played at least ten games. The losers had to take a shot each time they lost, and I didn't win a single round. After taking all of those shots, I got dizzy and felt the urge to lay down. "The sofa that you and Shay are sitting on can turn into a bed," Johaly confirmed as she told us to stand up. How I stood up without falling, I'll never know.

Even though it felt like the room was spinning, I continued to watch them play UNO. After losing another two rounds, Shay had enough too and joined me on the bed of the sofa couch. The last thing I remember was asking Johaly if there were any blankets in the pool house. When she pointed to the closet door near the bathroom, I crawled off the mattress to the door and reached inside. After I had pulled out a fuzzy peach blanket, I crawled back to the mattress on my hands and knees and lay down next to Shay. Just as I spread the blanket over my shivering body, Shay complained about being cold, so I slid closer to her and gave her a bit of the blanket.

My eyes fluttered in the dark room, and I wondered where I was. When I tried to turn over, I realized that someone was next to me. I rubbed my eyes, and one of my contacts shifted, as I blinked again and saw Shay's silhouette. I wondered where Leo and Johaly were as I tried to get comfortable. While drifting off again, I closed my eyes and remembered that Shay and I had shared a kiss. *"I kissed a girl! Holy shit. Did that really happen?"* The voice in my head asked. When I lifted the covers, I saw that I was naked, and she was too. I didn't know what to do, so I woke her up.

"Shay, wake up."

"I've got a hangover from out of this world," she said as she turned over and looked at me.

"What in the hell happened? Did we have sex?" I asked with a confused look on my face.

"Well, duh. Why else would the both of us be in bed naked together?"

I started to hyperventilate, as I tried to sit up in the bed.

"But, Shay. I'm not gay. I don't like girls."

"I'm not either, but from what you did to me last night, I might be now. You made me feel like I was a virgin all over again. Being with you was different, and you're so soft," she confessed as she quickly kissed me on the cheek and got out of the bed.

As I tried to piece together the events that had taken place last night, I couldn't. It was all too blurry. "Do you want to take a shower with me before I go?" She inquired from the small bathroom.

"I don't think that would be a good idea," I murmured as I watched her walk towards me.

"Aw, come on. It'll be fun, I promise."

Since I'd already got down and dirty with her last night, there was no reason that I couldn't get clean with her this morning.

In the shower, the hot water rained down on the both of us. Our bodies rubbed slightly against one another as we bathed and rinsed off. I had to admit; I was getting turned on by this, and my nipples were erect. I didn't know what felt better, Shay's hands caressing every curve on my body or the grinding that she was doing on my ass. I was lost in a world of curiosity as she reached around me and turned off the water. I stepped out of the shower first, and she stepped out last. I started to say something about there being only one towel on the rack, but Shay solved that problem.

She grabbed the large beach type towel and wrapped us both up in it. We were face to face now, and I felt a little uncomfortable, but before I could say anything she kissed me. Her soft full lips felt like heaven, and I wanted more. After the towel had fallen to the floor, I pulled her towards the bed, and we both settled under the covers.

"Can I make you feel like you made me felt last night?" She asked as she positioned herself on top of me. I wanted to speak, but I forgot how to at the moment, and only shook my head yes. She then parted my lips with her tongue and kissed me. I kissed her back the best I could until her head went a little lower and she sucked at my nipples.

I wanted to shout out, "Yes!" But I was afraid. I only yelled out things on the inside of my head until Shay's head moved a little lower. When she spread my legs open, I didn't stop her. She slipped one finger inside of me and I let out a delicate moan. My eyes opened as she inserted a few more fingers in and began to taste me. I came undone as she teased my clitoris with her tongue. While she searched deeper inside of my warmth, I moaned loudly and squeezed my toes together.

When she was finished, she licked her lips and cuddled up next to me. I wished that she had kissed me again, but she didn't, she only drifted off to sleep. While she slept, I watched her and wondered what I did to her last night. Little did she know, I was comparing her oral skills to Trevor's. Let me stop. There was no comparison. Trevor and Shay were the only two people on this Earth that ever went down on me. Hands down Shay out did Trevor. She even kissed better than him. The fire that she set inside of me that morning was still burning. Before I went back to sleep, I stole a kiss from her sweet lips and got as close to her as I could without waking her.

After another hour of sleep, Shay woke me up and said that she and Leo were about to leave. She bent down and kissed me on the lips one final time and told me goodbye. I was in a trance and rested in her warm spot as I heard voices coming from the backyard. As bad as I wanted to go back to sleep, I resisted the urge and put on my bikini that was beside the bed. When I opened the door of the pool house, I saw Leo and Johaly talking by the back porch. Shay was gathering a few of her extension cords that Leo didn't put in the van last night.

"Let me help you," I said as I walked over to her.

I picked up a long black cord and wrapped it in a circular shape, and the two of us walked towards the side of the house. I followed her to the back of the van and handed her the extension cord.

She smiled at me and said, "Last night, was fun. Maybe we can hang out again."

"I hope so. Hey, did I give you my number?"

"Yeah, I believe that you did. Let me check my phone."

While she looked at her phone, Leo and Johaly approached the van.

"Yeah, I got it. I'm going to call you this afternoon," she said.

"Okay, I'll be looking for your call."

Johaly gave Leo a hug before he climbed into the passenger seat of the van.

"Thanks for your help guys, we appreciate it," Johaly shouted as the van rolled away.

Leo and Shay waved their hands out of the window, and we both waved back.

"I slept with Leo," Johaly confessed.

"I slept with Shay."

"How was it? I've never been with a girl before, but I think I want to try it."

"It was different. A good different, though," I said with a giggle, then changed the subject, "Is Imani up?"

"Nope, that little heffa is still asleep," she confirmed as we walked around the house and entered the back door.

"So what are we going to eat for breakfast this morning?" I asked.

"We've got a pan of baked beans and six hot dogs. I can cook a pot of grits to go with that if you want me to."

"Yeah, I want some grits. Hopefully, it will soak up the rest of the alcohol that's in my system. I have a bit of a hangover, and I don't want to see another deck of UNO cards anytime soon."

Johaly laughed and started the pot of grits as soon as we walked into the kitchen. While she talked about the wild sex that she and Leo had, I shook my head and hoped that they didn't wake Imani up making all of that noise. Just as she heated up the baked beans and franks, she asked how I had rested. I replied, "I slept well, that pull out couch has a pretty good mattress."

8

Did I Do That?

Since Johaly had a hot date with Leo, I stayed at my mother's apartment tonight. After declining her invitation to go with her to play Bingo, she left with her lucky rabbit's foot and a bag of ink daubers. "Are you sure you don't want to go? There's a twenty thousand dollar jackpot tonight," she announced as she slid her feet into her worn leather sandals. "Nah, I don't feel like being around all of those people tonight. Good luck, though."

Now that she was gone, it was only Imani, Lester and I. After watching an episode of *Sister Sister*; Imani suggested that we all play a board game. She pulled out Monopoly and Trouble. After drinking two wine coolers, I didn't feel like counting money, so I chose the board game Trouble. I was surprised that Lester wanted to play, but happily gave him a rundown of the instructions for the game.

Before we started the game, Lester went to the kitchen and grabbed a beer.

"You ladies want something to drink?"

"I want some Kool-Aid," Imani ordered.

"Are there any wine coolers left?" I inquired.

He didn't say anything else before he returned with a glass of grape Kool-Aid and a strawberry wine cooler. Lester distributed our drinks and headed back to the kitchen. This time, when he came back, he had a bag of chips and a bowl of popcorn. He set the bowl down on the coffee table, and we all huddled around it.

We laughed, ate, and enjoyed one another's company until Imani fell asleep, in the middle of game three. She was passed out like she'd been sneaking sips of my wine coolers. Lester tried to wake her up, but there was no use. He ended up carrying her to her small room at the end of the hallway. While he was gone, I cleaned up the mess that we had made with the chips and popcorn. Just as I was about to put the game up Lester came back from down the hallway.

"You don't have to put the game up. I'd like to finish playing if you still want to." "I guess we can finish the game. I don't have anything else to do, and it's still early," I admitted as he sat back down. Lester and I never started playing the game again because he asked me a question. "So, what's it like to live in Texas?" From there I opened up to my new stepdad. I told him about my job, my students, and Trevor.

I was hesitant at first, and I knew that I hadn't even told my mom or Johaly about the entire Trevor situation. But, I told Lester. For some odd reason, I felt like he would keep my secrets and he was so easy to talk to. He listened and asked questions about everything. I'm not sure why I was telling him about this entire ordeal, but I felt much better after I let it all out.

"So you're telling me that you've only been with one man?"

I felt uneasy about where this conversation was going, but I answered it untruthfully because I just had sex with Manny the other night.

"Yeah, Trevor is the only man that I've ever been with."

"Would you be interested in making a little extra money tonight?" He asked with a devilish grin.

My heart pounded as I answered his question.

"Sure, I could use some extra dough. Do you need me to do some filing or something down at your office?"

"No, I've got an itch that needs to be scratched and only you can get the job done."

"Lester, I'm not going to have sex with you. What kind of woman do you think I am? You're my mother's husband for crying out loud."

Without giving him a chance to say anything else, I got up off of the floor and made my way to my bedroom door.

"You could make an easy two hundred dollars."

"Two hundred dollars! What would I have to do?" I said as I stopped dead in my tracks and turned around.

"I don't want to have sex with you. All I want is a hand job, and I would like you to watch a porn video with me."

"I don't know Lester. What if my mom catches us?"

"She won't, she never comes back from bingo before twelve. It's only ten-thirty. We've got at least an hour and a half. Come on sweetness."

Lester was getting excited already. I could tell because he had a gleam in his eye.

"Alright, I'll do it but, that's all. I'm not sucking it or anything else. Now get the porn so I can get this over with."

He happily stood up, turned the lights off, and put the lock on the apartment door.

"So where should we do this? In my room or in here?" I asked.

"Let's go in your room, do you have a DVD player in there?"

"Yeah, I have one."

"Alright, I'm going to check on Imani to make sure that she is still asleep, and I'll get the DVD."

"Alright," I replied as I went into my room.

"What in the hell did I just agree to?" I asked myself as I paced back and forth. I knew that I wasn't drunk, so why was I doing this. I tried talking myself out of it, but Lester walked in my room with a DVD in one hand and a wad of money in the other. After he had given me the money, I counted it.

"Lester, this is five hundred dollars."

"I know, I may let you keep the extra three hundred if you do a good job."

"Come on, let's get this over with," I said as I stuffed the money into my purse.

Lester took off his robe and pulled down his boxers before he sat on my bed.

"Hey, wait a minute. Let me get a towel or something before you blow your load all over my comforter."

After retrieving a towel from the bathroom across the hallway, I started the DVD player. I fast forwarded it to a scene and pressed play before I sat down beside him. He stroked his manhood as the two ladies on the screen pleasured each other. I watched the video quietly and thought about Shay. I had to admit I was getting moist and reached over to help Lester out without him asking me to.

His manhood was harder than a rock, and it was thick, black, and long. I'd never seen a penis this big before and wondered how it would feel inside of me. I stroked him in a delicate manner, and he fell back on the bed. "That feels so damn good," he whispered. I continued to watch the video and even played with Lester's balls until he spoke.

"Summer, do you think I can touch you?"

"Touch me how?"

"Take your panties off and I'll show you."

With my hormones raging, I took my panties off without hesitation. When I sat back down on the bed, he sat up and told me to lay down. I did as he said and closed my eyes. The bed shook a little as he positioned himself on top of me.

My legs were still closed at the moment. But when he told me to open them, I asked him to put on a condom.

"I'm not going to stick it in all the way. I only want to feel your wetness, and I don't have any condoms," he said.

"Well I do, get up. I'm not crazy. I know what's about to happen. As soon as you feel how tight and hot my juice box is you're going to want to go deeper."

Lester slid to the back side of the bed as I sat up and reached in my purse for a condom. I tore the package open and slid it onto his massive erection. Then I laid back down beside him, and he climbed on top of me again. While he positioned himself between my thighs, I felt his penis brush up against the lips of my vagina. I wanted to close my eyes, but I couldn't because the two girls that were on the video had my full attention.

His mustache tickled my neck as he kissed me and I almost burst out in a giggle. As I relaxed my legs fell open, and he stuck one of his short stubby fingers inside of me. I held my breath as he fingered me and I tried not to show any enjoyment, but it felt great. His erection poked me in my thigh as he continued to play in my love box.

"I'm going to enter you now if that's alright."

"Okay, I think I'm ready," I said as I shut my eyes.

He pushed inside with a bit of a struggle, and I took a deep breath.

"This hurts," I whispered.

"I'll do it slowly, just bear with me for a second."

When most of his erection was stuffed inside of me, I felt full. I didn't feel pleasure until he slowly pumped a few more times and my love juices squirted out. I couldn't control myself, and I thought that he had punctured my bladder as my vagina continued to leak.

The water fountain between my legs wouldn't stop flowing as he took longer and deeper strokes. When the bed began to squeak, it really got good, and I had to put a pillow over my face so I wouldn't wake Imani. He hit all the right spots, and I was speechless.

In a way, I felt like I should be paying him for this experience. When he climaxed, he withdrew himself and took off the condom. It felt like he'd left a gaping hole where his monster cock had been. As my breathing returned to normal, I reached down and felt the bed, and there was a large wet spot underneath my body. I had no idea that I was capable of squirting. I saw women do it before on porn videos, but never in real life. I wondered if Trevor would want to marry me if he knew I could do this.

Before I could think another thought. Lester said, "You got some good stuff in between those legs little lady. That Trevor is a fool. If I were twenty years younger, I would marry you," he joked as he pulled his pajama pants up and ejected the DVD from the player.

"Thanks, yeah he is a fool. Hey, do you think that we could do this again?"

"I'm not sure if that would be a good idea, Summer. I'd better go shower before your mother gets home. It's almost twelve."

"Okay, I could use a shower too."

That was the last thing I said before I fell asleep naked in the wet spot on my bed. I was dreaming about swimming in the ocean when a loud commotion woke me up. I jumped up and immediately thought that my mother knew what Lester and I had done while she was gone, but that wasn't the case. "I won, I won!" I heard her shout as I put on my robe and tied the belt. When I peeked my head out of my bedroom door, I saw that the light was on in the living room. Just as I was about to come out, Lester walked by.

"Baby, what's going on?" He asked as she jumped up and hugged him.

"I won the jackpot at bingo tonight."

"You did? That's wonderful. How much did you win?"

"The entire thing, twenty thousand dollars."

She then sat down on the couch and pulled out a check.

"See here it is," she shouted as I came out into the living room.

"What's going on? Is everything okay?" I asked.

"Your Mom won the jackpot. Look at this check," Lester said as he passed the rectangular sheet of paper in my direction.

"Oh my God! Mom this is fantastic!"

While the two of them hugged and jumped up and down, I wished that I would have gone to bingo with my mother instead of staying here and sleeping with her husband tonight. I could have won that money. God knows I sure needed it. As the wheels turned in my head, I wondered if she was going to offer me any of her winnings. I was almost certain that she was, but I was going to let her ask me before I said a word.

"I'm going to start a pot of coffee and cook some breakfast," Mom said before she walked towards the kitchen.

Lester followed close behind her and didn't look back to see if I was going to join them or not. I thought about going back to bed, but I figured that I wouldn't get much sleep with all the excitement in the air. Just as I was about to go into the kitchen, Imani came out of her room and asked what was going on. When I told her about the big win, she jumped up and down and left me standing in the living room all alone.

Even though I didn't feel like smiling, I slapped on a fake grin and sat down at the table across from Lester. While mom told us every last detail about what happened at the bingo hall, I looked around the small kitchen and tuned her out. She had been living in this apartment for almost twelve years. I remembered the day that we moved into this place. When I say we, I'm talking about my mom, my daddy, and myself. They were engaged for the longest, but never got married, and it was a good thing too because they used to fight like cats and dogs.

Our last residence had two bedrooms, but it was in a bad part of the city, that's why we moved to this complex. While my father was at work, my mother looked for apartments. Without him knowing, she checked out a couple of three bedroom apartments and told my father everything about this place except for the extra bedroom. I remember him complaining about how high the rent was as we pulled up to the complex. It was only an additional twenty-five dollars a month, but I guess back then that was a lot of money.

Before we could get the furniture moved into this place they fought, right in the middle of the living room. My dad, God rest his soul, was one of the cheapest men on this planet and didn't realize that the lease he signed was for a three bedroom apartment. For some reason, my mother always wanted a guest room, but we never had any company stay over. That day my mom got her guest bedroom, and she got a black eye to go along with it.

"Summer, do you want bacon or sausage?"

My mother asked me for a second time.

"Oh, sorry Mom, I was in a daze. I'll take a few pieces of bacon."

"I hope you're not thinking about your wedding. Now that I have this extra money, I can afford to buy an elegant dress to wear. Maybe we can go to that fancy dress shop at the mall sometime this week."

While she piled strips of crispy bacon on my plate, I lost my appetite when she reminded me of the wedding. Lester looked at me, and I looked away, he knew that as of right now there was no wedding. I had to tell my mother about the split, and I had to tell her soon. Maybe I would tell her this week before she went shopping for a dress. I let out a deep breath as she set my plate down in front of me.

After drinking a few cups of coffee, I couldn't keep my eyes off of Lester. Even though his plaid robe was closed tightly, I wondered if he had on anything underneath it. While he and my mom talked about going out to eat at the barbecue restaurant downtown, I remembered the orgasm that he had given me only hours earlier in my room. I wanted him again and hoped that he and mom weren't going to have sex tonight. If they did, I sure as hell didn't want to hear them.

After barely eating my food, I left the kitchen. I closed my bedroom door and listened to the muffled voices coming through the thin wall as I tried to get comfortable in the bed. The damp spot in the center of the mattress from the sex session hadn't dried yet, and I was forced to go to the linen closet for fresh sheets. After I had stripped my bed of the damp covers, I left the pile of soiled bedding on the floor. Then I put a clean towel over the wet spot on the mattress before I made my bed.

Before I got in bed, I grabbed my phone from the nightstand. It had been hooked up to the charger for the last four hours and it was hot to the touch. *"I hope that I didn't do any damage to the battery by leaving it plugged in for so long,"* I thought to myself as I looked at my call log. "Damn," I had missed calls from Mark, Johaly, and Shay. After looking at the clock and seeing that it was a little after three in the morning, I knew that it was too late to call anybody back now. So I covered myself up and watched television until I fell asleep.

9

Bingo!

The next morning I woke up a little after eleven. After stretching and yawning, I realized that the house was quiet. *"Maybe everyone was still asleep,"* I thought as I reached for my cell phone on the nightstand. I had another missed call from Johaly; I figured all she wanted to do was tell me about her date with Leo and the message on my voicemail confirmed that I was right. Since I already knew that she was okay, I called Mark.

"Hello," he answered.

"Hey Mark, I'm sorry that I missed your call last night. Things got pretty crazy," I said before I could catch myself.

"That's okay. I was only calling to check on you, but it seems like you're having fun. Everything is going well isn't it?"

I fell silent before I replied because I hadn't been in touch with him like I should've been. Considering that I hadn't heard from Trevor, I needed to keep up with Mark. He just may be my only friend in Texas, and I didn't want to lose him.

"Yeah. Things are great. My mom won the big jackpot at the bingo hall last night, and we were up late celebrating."

"Oh, that's wonderful. I wish that I was that lucky."

"I won a few hundred bucks on a scratch-off too," I added.

"What? Maybe I need to come to Miami," he replied with a chuckle.

After talking to Mark, I felt like I missed him. We had only known each other for a few weeks, and I was wondering if this was something normal. I didn't know how I was supposed to feel, being in a relationship with Trevor for so long had me messed up. Thinking about him reminded me that I would have to tell my mother about the break up sooner than later. Now that she had that check, I knew that it was going to burn a hole in her pocket, and she would want to go shopping for that dress much sooner than later.

Over the next few days, I didn't hang out with Johaly even though she begged me to come over. After hearing all the hot and heavy details about her and Leo, my hormones were raging, and I needed sex. If I left the apartment, I feared that I would give up my goodies to the next tall, dark, and handsome man I saw. I tried to stay in my room whenever Lester came home from work. I didn't want to be anywhere around him. Even sitting across from him turned me on. I loved the way that he chewed with his mouth closed and the way his bald head glistened under the light fixture hanging from the ceiling in the kitchen.

While I admired my stepfather, Imani slurped down her sweet tea and bugged him about staying the night with one of her friends tomorrow. "I'll think about it," he said in a stern voice, and that was the end of the conversation. While we all finished our dinner quietly, my mother made the announcement.

"I'm going to look at a few houses tomorrow, Lester. There are three for sale in this neighborhood."

"That's great. I may be able to take a few hours off in the morning and go with you," he replied.

"A new house! I can't wait. I hope that I have a bigger room," Imani said.

"Don't get your hopes up baby. I'll have to get approved for the loan first, and the houses that we're going to look at aren't new. People have lived in them before," my mother said.

"That's fine. It will be new to us. Ain't that right Daddy?"

"That's right baby."

I got up from the table and said, "That's great, I'm sure that you guys will find something beautiful."

"I'm confident that we will," Lester said as he watched me put my plate in the sink.

After I had walked down the short hall, I went into my room and got on the bed. He wanted me. I could see the lust in his eyes. The way he eyeballed my legs when I was standing in front of the kitchen sink set my soul on fire. I wanted him, and I had to feel his thick blessing between my legs again. I was a burning ball of fire and had to do something to cool myself off, so I took a cold shower.

I felt a little better and went to bed naked. I made sure that I locked my door because I knew that Imani would barge in on me if I didn't. Just as I reached over to turn the lamp off on the nightstand, Mark crossed my mind. With high hopes, I called him and waited for him to answer. When I heard his voice, I felt a funny feeling in the pit of my stomach. We only talked for a few minutes because he was on his way to hang out with a few of his new friends from the police department.

After we had got off the phone, I put the pillow over my head and tried to make myself go to sleep. Just as my eyelids came to a close, I heard a knock on my room door.

"Imani, go away. You're not sleeping in here tonight," I said without moving the pillow from over my face. "It's not Imani. It's me," my mother answered. Before I unlocked the door, I put on a sports bra and a pair of pajama bottoms.

"What's up Mom?" I asked as I sat down at the foot of the bed.

"Summer, I know that something is bothering you. You're my child, and I can tell these things."

"I'm okay," I lied.

"No, you're not, I'm not leaving this room until you tell me what's going on."

After taking a deep breath, I prayed to God for a brief second and hoped that this conversation had nothing to do with Lester.

"Alright Mom, I'll tell you what's going on."

Before I could say anything else, she asked, "What did Trevor do? I know that he did something to you? I'm going to kill his ass."

"How did you know?" I asked as my eyes filled with tears.

"You haven't been saying much about him. You usually brag about him doing this and that for you, but I've heard nothing about him since you've been here. I haven't even seen you on the phone with him."

I was tired of beating around the bush and told my mother everything. My throat felt thick as I started to talk, "He said that he needed a break, but he's already dating a girl that lives in our apartment complex."

"That little no good son of a ..."

Before she could finish her sentence, words flew from my mouth like I was singing a song.

"I don't think that there is going to be a wedding either. I lied about the invitations. The printer didn't make a mistake with them. They've been sitting on the shelf gathering dust this entire time. I'm sorry Mom."

"My poor baby."

She leaned in and gave me a hug before she went across the hall and got some tissue.

When she returned, I dried the tears from my cheeks before she asked, "So how are you dealing with this?"

"At first, I thought that the world was going to end. I was overwhelmed and stressing like crazy. I don't believe that it's as bad now, though. I'm not going to lie. I still love Trevor, and I hope that we get married."

"Darling, I can understand that. I hate that you have to go through this. Just remember that you can tell me anything. I'm your mother, and I'm not going to judge you."

That night I told her every single thing that happened between Trevor and me. She was furious when she found out that he broke it off with me over the phone. And when she found out that he had taken all the furniture she almost blew her top. I had to keep telling her to calm down and to get her mind off of Trevor; I told her about Mark. She listened inquisitively as she asked questions and took a liking to him immediately.

After talking about Mark for almost thirty minutes, somehow the subject changed, and we started talking about the houses that she was going to view tomorrow.

"You should come house hunting with us."

"I have an appointment at the nail spa in the morning," I lied.

When the look on my mother's face changed, I wanted to take the lie back, but it was too late.

"Well, whenever you're done at the nail place, you can meet up with us. Maybe Lester will take us out to lunch or something."

"Okay, that sounds like a plan."

Before she left my room, she gave me another hug and told me that she loved me. I felt like a piece of shit. How could I do my mother like this? I had to get Lester off of my mind and quick. Having sex with him was wrong on so many levels, and I had to get him out of my system. I think I could muster up the willpower to steer clear of him. I only had a few more weeks of fun in the sun, and my vacation would be over.

When I got back in the bed, I turned the television off. My eyes searched around the dimly lit room as I thought about Trevor. Where in the hell was he and why hasn't he been answering my calls? In a way, I didn't want to know. I had a bad feeling about this Trevor situation. Just as I turned over, my thoughts switched from Trevor to my mother. Maybe I would go with them to look at some houses tomorrow. I was very happy for her because she'd never lived in a house her entire life. Her parents always lived in an apartment, and we'd always lived in an apartment as well. When I thought about it. Everybody in our family lived in some sort of dwelling that was connected to another dwelling. Be it an apartment, condo, townhouse, or duplex.

The dream that I had about Lester was so realistic that I woke up looking to see if he was in my bed. My heart pounded as my mother knocked on the door and told me that breakfast was ready. "Okay," I said as I sat up. I heard Lester's deep voice as he and my mother talked about something in the kitchen. I debated about joining them because I didn't want to see him. With the smell of the bacon calling my name, I couldn't resist and washed my face quickly before I headed to the kitchen. After telling everyone good morning, I kept my head down and didn't make any contact with Lester.

As they talked excitedly about looking at the houses, I gobbled down my food and popped open a can of Dr. Pepper only to break one of my nails. "Shit," I cursed as I immediately put my finger in my mouth and prayed silently that it wasn't bleeding. My finger throbbed as I took it out of my mouth to look at it. The nail was broken, but my finger wasn't bleeding. It looked like I was going to have to go to the nail spa today after all. While I sucked my finger, Lester looked at me with hungry eyes. I saw that he was watching me and sucked on my finger a little more.

"Ooh, Summer said a bad word," Imani snitched.

"Sorry guys," I said as I got up from the table to excuse myself.

"Imani, you'd curse too if that happened to you. That mess hurts. That's exactly why I don't wear false nails anymore. I popped my nail off one day when I was trying to open a car door, and I almost passed out."

Mom was right. I felt like saying a few more explicit words, but I kept them to myself as I went into the bathroom and ran cold water over my finger. As soon as I opened the bathroom door, Imani was standing there.

"Can I go with you to Johaly's house today?"

"No ma'am, not today."

"Why not?"

"Because, you've been hanging out with us too much. I thought you were going house shopping with Lester and Mom?"

"I want to go with them, and I want to stay with you."

"I'll tell you what, we can hang out together when you come back. I may not even go to Johaly's today."

"Okay, I'm going to pack an overnight bag just in case dad changes his mind about letting me stay with my friend. I will see you when we get back because I have a feeling that he's going to say no again."

"Good luck."

With Imani out of my hair, I called the nail spa and made an appointment to get my nail fixed.

I put on a pair of homemade shorts with a white tank top and left the house before everyone else did. Just when I shut the door to the apartment, Lester opened it and said, "I can give you a ride to the nail spa." Without turning around, I declined his offer and kept on walking. After I crossed the street and walked a couple of blocks, I passed a few houses that had for sale signs in the yards and wondered if these were the houses that my mother had told us about.

When I reached the nail spa, my shirt was drenched with sweat. I wished that I had taken Lester up on his offer because I felt like I was about to faint. The door of the nail spa was wide open, and I could smell the fumes from the acrylic and nail polish before I walked in. I didn't know how the workers inhaled this stuff on a daily basis. This couldn't be good for their lungs.

I was on time for my appointment, but I still had to wait twenty minutes. The nail salon was jammed packed with women of all ages, colors, and sizes. Some ladies held their babies while they got their nails done. When it was my turn, I sat in the chair at nail station number six. After telling the nail technician that I needed a repair, she asked me if I wanted to get my nails polished too. After looking at the boring french tips, I agreed to let her paint them a bright yellow color after she repaired my nail. My phone rang as the young lady put a second coat of polish on my nails. I wanted to answer it and thought that it may have been Trevor calling, but I couldn't risk messing my nails up.

It didn't take very long for her to get me fixed up and I was out of the door in no time. When I left the nail spa, I had forgotten about the missed calls and purchased a frozen lemonade from the juice bar on the next block over. While I sipped the refreshing beverage, I admired my nails until I heard a horn blow.

"Hey, hot stuff. Can I give you a lift?"

When I turned around, I saw that it was Johaly. She was driving her aunt's convertible. I walked a little faster as she stopped in the middle of the road and backed up. I was glad that there weren't any cars coming because what she was doing was illegal. I laughed as I approached the car and carefully opened the door because the thought of my mother's horrible nail story entered my mind.

"Where have you been? It's too hot to be out here walking."

"I had to get my nail fixed. I broke it this morning when I tried to open a can of soda. I didn't want to bother you. I figured that you might have been asleep."

"I was asleep. I stayed over at Leo's last night, and he wore my ass out again."

"Are you guys a couple now or what?"

"Girl, I don't know. I'm just having fun. Oh, that reminds me, we're going out tonight. Shay invited us to this hot new strip club that she's going to be deejaying at. She said that she was going to call and invite you."

"I missed a few calls when I was at the nail spa this morning. I'll check my messages whenever I get home. I think my nails are dry, but I don't feel comfortable digging in my purse just yet."

"Was the nail spa packed?"

"Packed isn't the word."

"I want a pedicure. Leo tried to suck my toes last night, and I wouldn't even let him look at them," she said with a giggle. "If you don't have anything else to do, I'd like to treat you to a pedicure."

"That sounds good to me," I said as she made a U-turn in the middle of the street.

My hair blew in the wind as I finished off my lemonade. A part of me wanted to tell her about what happened between Lester and me, but I wasn't sure of how she'd react so I kept my lips buttoned.

When we reached the nail spa, most of the waiting customers had left. After she selected the polish she wanted, we sat down in the last two available pedicure chairs. Luckily they were beside each other. We didn't say much as the roller on the back of the massage chairs rolled up and down our backs. I felt like I would fall asleep as the same young lady who had fixed my nail earlier scrubbed my feet. When she asked if I wanted the same color that I had on my fingernails, I shook my head yes and shut my eyes.

Just then I remembered that I needed to check my messages on my phone. I knew that my nails had to be dry now. As I carefully reached in my purse, I saw that I had two missed calls from Shay and a missed call from Trevor. Instead of checking the messages, I put the phone back in my purse and enjoyed the rest of my pedicure. An hour later we were pulling in front of my mother's apartment complex. I thought about the talk that my mother and I had last night until Johaly asked, "Are you sure you don't want to come to my house?"

"Yes. I'm sure. I'm tired. I think I'm going to take a nap. That massage did something to me."

"Okay, did you ever decide if you want to go to the club tonight?"

"I'm not sure. I'll call you when I wake up and let you know."

"Alright."

After I let myself into the apartment, I collapsed on the couch and called Trevor. When he didn't answer, I left a brief message and hoped that he would call back soon. Then I called Shay. She was happy to hear from me and told me about the club that she was going to be working at tonight. I'd never been to a strip club, and I didn't want anybody shaking any of their body parts in my face. Shay laughed after I made that comment and insisted that it wasn't like that. While she tried to tell me what I should expect, I got a little too comfortable on the couch and fell asleep in the middle of our conversation.

10

Sensual Seduction

When I heard the door slam, I opened my eyes to see my mother standing in front of me. My heart immediately dropped because I thought that she was going to say something about what Lester and I had done the other night.

"Summer, we found the perfect house. We put an offer in, now we're waiting to hear back from the realtor. All it needs is some fresh paint and new carpet. Lester said that he would take a few days off work to fix it up before we move in. That's if the owner accepts our offer."

"That's wonderful. I can't wait to see it. Where is Lester anyway?" I asked as I sat up and yawned.

"He's dropping Imani off at one of her friend's house. He finally agreed to let her stay the night."

"I know she's happy. I'm glad that he finally let her stay."

"Me too, because the poor child has been asking for weeks."

"You and Dad used to do me the same way. I used to ask to stay the night with Johaly all the time. Don't you remember?"

Mom let out a laugh, and said, "Yes. I sure do. I'm sorry pumpkin."

"That's okay. So I guess that it's just going to be us three tonight then. I was invited to a club, but I don't think I'm going to go."

"No ma'am, you and Lester will be here. I'm going to press my luck at bingo again. The Jackpot is up to five thousand dollars. Maybe I can win that," she said as she scooted into the kitchen.

Lester and I are going to have the house all to ourselves tonight, the voice in my head squealed. I couldn't believe it. I was going to get him. There's no way he would be able to resist me. I started a bubble bath while my mother fried pork chops in the kitchen. The food smelled amazing, but I wanted to bathe and shave before I tried to seduce Lester. There was no way he would be able to turn down a freshly shaved cooch and a sweet smelling oiled body.

Just as I was finishing up in the bathroom, mom knocked at the door; then announced that she was about to go to bingo. I wished her good luck, then I heard the entry door to the apartment shut, and I came out of the bathroom. Lester still wasn't back yet. I didn't know what was taking him so long. While I decided on how I would seduce him, the thought of sitting on the couch with my satin robe open crossed my mind.

I looked out of the window to see if his car was in the parking lot and it wasn't. The street lamps had just flickered on, and a few children scurried into the downstairs apartments as the sun began to set. Just as I closed the blind and sucked my teeth, my stomach started to growl. With him nowhere in sight, I went to the kitchen to eat. After I had filled my plate with fried pork chop, rice, corn, and stewed tomatoes, I sat down. Just as I took a bite of the perfectly seasoned pork chop, I heard the door of the apartment open.

"Is anybody home?" Lester asked.

I quickly chewed and swallowed the food that was in my mouth and answered, "Yes, I am. I'm in the kitchen."

"It sure smells good in here, I'm hungry, but I've got to get out of these sweaty clothes. Can you fix a plate for me and put it in the microwave?"

"Sure," I answered with a smile.

When Lester went into the room and shut the door, I quickly ate my food, fixed his plate, made sure the door to the apartment was locked, lit a few candles, and brushed my teeth. After I had turned on some old school music, I opened my hot pink satin robe and sat on the couch. My heart thumped when I heard the shower turn off because I knew that Lester would be coming out of the room soon, and I was nervous.

When the door opened from down the hall, I sat up straight. My perky breasts and erect nipples stood at attention as I took a deep breath. I was almost afraid to look up, but I talked myself into doing so, just as he turned the corner. When our eyes met, I slowly blinked and bit my bottom lip. He stood speechless as I opened my legs and asked, "How would you like a massage? I know you had a stressful day house hunting."

"Where are your clothes?" He asked as he walked over and sat down beside me on the couch.

"Don't worry about that. Don't you like what you see?"

"Hell yes! I love it, but this is wrong."

"What my mother doesn't know won't hurt her," I said as I stood up and straddled his lap.

With my breasts directly in front of his face, he couldn't resist and started licking my nipples.

The thin material of his pajamas couldn't hide his excitement as his thickness began to rise. I could feel myself growing moist as he continued to suck at my breasts. Meanwhile, the hardness between my legs throbbed, and there was a wet spot on the front of his light blue pajama bottoms.

While he sucked greedily on my breasts, he asked, "I thought you said that you were going to give me a massage?"

"How could I forget about your massage?" I playfully questioned, as I stood up and said, "Take your pajamas off."

After he had followed my instructions, he sat back down on the couch. I then knelt down between his legs and looked at his manhood. It was large and in charge, and it also resembled a dark chocolate eggplant. Before I took his thickness into my mouth, I massaged it in my hands until a sticky clear liquid appeared. Then

I gathered the saliva from the cheeks of my mouth and let it dribble onto the head of his penis while he leaned his head back and moaned with satisfaction.

As my warm saliva slid down the shaft of his erection, I licked around the tip and took him deep in my mouth. I sucked and slurped on his blessing as he watched me with wide eyes. I thought that his eyes were going to pop out when his penis hit my tonsils, and I didn't gag. At the end of his massage I got up and kissed him on the lips, then I turned around and straddled his lap in the reverse cowgirl position. This time, it didn't hurt as bad, and when he was all the way inside I moved up and down slowly.

"I hope you know that this can't happen again," he said at the end of a groan.

"You've got to be shitting me?" I answered just as I was getting into the groove.

"Summer, this isn't right."

"I know it isn't. But it feels so damn good," I said as I tightened the muscles in my pelvis.

He didn't say anything else after that. Then I climaxed and squirted all over his lap as his hands came alive. After he had slapped me on my right butt cheek a few times, he grabbed at my ass and attempted to stick one of his fingers in my butthole. I felt a hot sensation all over my body as I continued to ride his erection. When his finger made its way to my hot spot, I let out a moan and Lester held onto my waist with one hand. I wanted to scream, but I didn't because I feared the neighbors would hear us.

"I'm gonna cum."

"Wait, let me get up," I said before I jumped up off of his lap.

Cum shot straight up in the air. It got on the coffee table and some even squirted on my bare ass and robe. I laughed while Lester looked at me.

"What are you trying to do to me?" He asked in a serious tone.

"Whatever you want me to do to you, I guess."

"Your mom is going to kill both of us if she finds out. You know that don't you?"

"She's not going to find out, plus I'll be going back to Texas soon."

"Alright, my lips are sealed. I will take this secret to my grave. I promise."

"Same here," I replied as I blew the candles out.

As soon as Lester got up off the couch, I removed the damp cushion and shoved it in the dryer with a dryer sheet. Then I called Johaly and told her that I wanted to go to the party and asked her what time she was coming to pick me up. After looking at the clock, I realized that I only had about thirty minutes to get ready, so I showered, dressed, and reminded Lester to take the couch cushion out of the dryer before I left.

On the way to the club, I couldn't help but think about what had happened with Lester back at the apartment. With him giving in to me tonight, I felt my feelings getting stronger for him and decided that it would be best if I stayed with Johaly for a few nights. Maybe the fire that burned for him inside of me would subside if I didn't see him for a couple of days.

"Why are you so quiet?"

"I was just thinking about how my life will be when I return to Texas," I lied.

"You still haven't heard anything from Trevor?"

"He called earlier when I was at the nail spa, but I missed his call, and he didn't leave a message."

"Did you call him back?"

"Yes. I did, and he didn't answer. I left him a message."

"Don't worry he'll call back." She said as she parked and we got out of the car.

After waiting in line for a few minutes, Johaly called Leo on his cell phone. Within a matter of seconds, we saw him talking to the bouncers. When he pointed in our direction, one of the bouncers motioned for us to come to the front of the line. Mean girls yelled obscenities as we happily trotted by them in our miniskirts and high heels. We ignored them with a smile and showed our identification to the bouncers and Leo took us inside.

The club was bumping. Bright lights flashed, and music pumped from the speakers. A smile spread across my face when Leo pointed to Shay up in the deejay booth. When she saw us, she waved and gave us a shout out over the microphone. I beamed with excitement as I blew her a kiss and we headed to the bar. As Leo and Johaly headed to the stage to get a closer look at the strippers, I sat on the stool and waved to get the bartender's attention.

"Excuse me," I shouted as I waved.

"Yes ma'am," she said with bright eyes.

"Can I please order a Mai Tai?"

"You can have whatever you'd like."

"Thanks," I said as I smiled.

When she returned with my drink, I tried to pay her with a ten dollar bill, but she didn't take it.

"All of your drinks are on the house tonight," she said after she winked at me.

"Are you serious?"

"Yes, but only if you promise to dance with me when the deejay plays my song."

"Alright," I replied as I took a sip of my drink.

I don't know why, but I felt comfortable with the beautiful bartender. It was something about her that I was attracted to. It may have been her smile, or it may have been the free drinks that she gave me. After downing four Mai Tai's and two shots of tequila, I had to go to the restroom, and I asked her where it was.

"I'll take you," she said. "I have to get dressed anyway. It will be my turn to dance soon."

"Dance? You're a stripper?"

"Yeah, and a bartender."

"That's pretty cool."

"I'm sorry, I didn't get your name back at the bar."

"My name is Summer."

"It's nice to meet you. My government name is Dawn, but my stripper name is D-Light," she said with a giggle and then added, "Do you strip too?"

"No! I don't have the guts to do that."

"You'd be surprised what you'd do if the price were right or if enough liquor was flowing through your bloodstream."

"I guess you're right."

"Hell yeah, I'm right!" She shouted as we rounded a corner.

As we walked through the club, I looked up at the deejay booth and saw that Shay was busy. I wished that I could join her, but the booth looked tiny from where I was standing, and I didn't want to distract her while she was working. The closer we got to the restrooms, the more my bladder felt like it was about to release its contents. After walking down an extra-long hallway we finally reached the restrooms, and I went into the first available stall.

I waited for Dawn as she washed her hands and we left. I thought that we were taking a shortcut back to the bar, but we ended up in the dressing room. As soon as she opened the door, I saw all types of girls. They were tall, short, thick, thin, light, white, black, and brown. Some were covered in tattoos and looked like they were in a gang, and others looked as innocent as the ushers at the church I attended when I was a child. While a few wore weaves or wigs, I saw one that had a fade, just like Trevor had.

I wonder what made her cut her hair in that particular style. *"Was her hair damaged? Was she going through something? Was she gay? Or did her stylist leave her relaxer in for too long?"* Whatever the case, I'll never know because she not only looked tough. She looked mean as a hornet. I took my attention away from the almost bald stripper when Dawn stopped walking, and I bumped into the back of her.

"Are you okay?" She asked as she pulled out a key and unlocked a locker.

"Oh, yeah. I'm sorry. I've never been in the dressing room of a strip club before."

"It's a lot to take in. It's a lot of ass and titties. Right?"

"Right," I answered with a smile and nod.

"So which outfit should I wear?" She asked as she held up two outfits that looked small enough to fit Imani.

"Um, I guess the black one."

"Okay."

Without any type of warning, she pulled her clothes off right in front of me. She had a voluptuous body, and I was a little jealous of her. I watched her carefully as she put on a stretchy lace outfit and high heels. Then she put the clothes that she previously wore inside of her locker, and grabbed a medium sized makeup bag.

I sat on the bench in front of her locker and watched her as she put on eyeshadow, face powder, lipstick, and lip gloss. Before she zipped the bag shut, she reached in and pulled out a bottle of glitter body spray and sprayed it all over herself. When she was all dolled up, she shoved the bag back in the locker and handed me the small set of keys.

"Can you hang on to these for me?"

"Sure," I said as I pushed the keys down into my bra.

"Are you about to perform now?"

"Nah, I've got about twenty more minutes. Let's go back to the bar. I need another drink."

On the way to the bar, I looked up to see what Shay was doing, and she was looking down at me. She could have been looking at Dawn because she looked hot in her stripper attire. I waved at her real quick as she motioned for me to come to her. Since I had no clue on how to get to the deejay booth, I held up one finger to tell her that I'll come up in a minute. She shook her head and smiled I wondered what she wanted.

When we approached the bar, there was only one stool available. I told Dawn that she could sit down, but she insisted that I have the stool. Maybe she didn't want to sit her bare ass on the cold seat. I wasn't sure, and I didn't ask her why because the other bartender handed Dawn a shot and she gave me one as well. We downed the shot with ease and swallowed another before I remembered that Shay was waiting for me.

"Dawn, how do you get to the deejay booth?"

"Do you see those stairs?" She asked as she pointed to a corner near the bar.

"Yeah. I see them."

"Okay. Take those stairs and make a left at the top. Are you Shay's girlfriend or something?"

"Girlfriend? No, we're only friends."

"Yeah, right," she laughed as the bartender handed her another shot.

On the way up the stairs, I wondered what in the hell Dawn was talking about. I wasn't Shay's girlfriend. I hope that she hadn't been telling people that. As I made a left at the top of the stairs, I saw Shay in the deejay booth. It was extremely loud up here, so I had to yell her name to get her attention. She wasn't startled, but I sure was when she turned around and kissed me.

"Damn, baby. You look incredible. I've been trying to keep my eye on you. Where have you been?"

I was shocked from the kiss, but what shocked me the most is the way I kissed her back. Was I under the influence of too much alcohol? Or is this something that I've been yearning for?

"Thank you. I went to the restroom; then Dawn showed me the dressing room."

"Okay, y'all were gone for a minute. I thought that she was giving you a private dance or something," she joked.

"Nah, nothing like that."

"Well I got to get back in the booth, this song is getting ready to end, and I need to introduce the next dancer. I only wanted to see you up close and taste those sweet lips of yours."

Then she moved in closer and kissed me again before asking, "Can you wait for me at the bar after I make the last call for alcohol?"

I blushed as I responded, "I sure can. Are you going to take me home? I rode here with Johaly, and I haven't seen her or Leo since they left me at the bar a few hours ago."

"They're in a private room getting a dance. I saw them go in there a few minutes ago. I can see everything from up here," she answered before she walked back towards the deejay booth.

My heart fluttered as I turned around and headed back to the staircase. I felt a little light headed as I thought about the kiss that we just shared. I held onto the black metal rail and smiled to myself. Had Shay been drinking too? Did she tell Dawn that I was her girlfriend? What in the hell was I getting myself into? That was the last thought that crossed my mind before I reached the bar where Dawn was standing.

She was still drinking shots and offered me one too. I accepted her offer and drank the shot with no problem.

"I didn't think you were coming back."

"Of course, I was coming back. I told you that I would be."

"I saw you up there being lovie-dovie with your girlfriend. That's so sweet."

"I told you before that Shay isn't my girlfriend. She's just a friend."

"If she's not your girlfriend then kiss me."

"What? Kiss you?"

"Yes. Kiss me."

Without looking up to see if Shay was watching, I leaned in and placed a kiss on Dawn's lips. Then she grabbed me and forced her tongue into my mouth. I didn't kiss her back the way I kissed Shay, but I did enjoy it.

"Are you happy now?" I asked as I licked my lips.

"No. I won't be happy until you make it rain on me."

"What in the hell did make it rain mean?" I thought to myself. I clearly remembered some of my students singing a song about making it rain, but I didn't know what that meant. Did she want me to pee on her? I couldn't finish thinking because Dawn put a small bucket filled with stacks of one dollar bills into my arms and started dragging me towards the stage.

"Where are we going?"

"I'm getting ready to dance. You're going to stand right here and throw this money at me while I dance. When the men see you throwing money, they'll throw more money because their egos won't allow a woman to outdo them."

"Oh, okay. I get it."

"I may pull you on stage. So make sure you're prepared."

"Alright."

"Wait a minute. Did she say that she was going to pull me on stage? Oh my God." I thought as she quickly walked away and the lights started to flash. A moment later the intro to French Montana's *Pop That* started to play, and I saw Dawn enter from the left side of the stage. The men were like hound dogs and howled as she dropped low and shook her rear end.

When she approached my side of the stage, I dug in the bucket and started throwing money just like she told me too. The more money I threw, the more Dawn humped the floor and opened her legs wide. When she climbed the pole, I was in awe of her skills and wanted to try some of those moves myself. Now the stage was covered with money, and she couldn't walk without stepping on dollar bills.

My heart almost exploded in my chest when she moved closer to me. When she shimmied her double D's in my face, I tossed more money up on the stage and so did the men that were standing around me. I couldn't believe that all the attention was on us as a spotlight fell on top of my head. After I had thrown the last few dollars that were in the bucket I was holding, I dropped it on the floor.

When I didn't have any money to throw, I didn't know what was about to happen. That's when Dawn walked off the stage and took me by the hand. I was so nervous that I thought I was going to pass out. The crowd roared even louder as she grabbed a chair from a table. I grinned from ear to ear as I followed her onto the stage. When she put the chair down, she pushed me down in it and started giving me a lap dance.

She wiggled and rubbed up against me in such a sexual manner that my mouth got dry. When I tried to swallow, my tongue got stuck to the roof of my mouth. If I had been a man, I would have had an erection. Not only were my panties wet, but my nipples were poking through the thin material of my shirt. I couldn't believe what was happening, and I not only needed another shot of tequila a.s.a.p., I needed someone to pinch me because I thought that I was dreaming.

11

Oops, I Did it Again

The next day I woke up with a terrible hangover. I had gotten so drunk at the club last night that I didn't even know where I was. I thought that I was in one of the spare bedrooms at Johaly's but quickly realized that I wasn't when I saw a huge painting of a girl wearing headphones and working her magic on a set of turntables. Just as I turned to move a blinged-out disco ball hanging from the ceiling caught my eye, and I knew that I had to be with someone who loved music. When a delicate arm wrapped around my waist, I saw Shay's tattoo and knew where I was.

Thinking that she was still asleep, I tried to move her arm without waking her. As soon as I reached for her arm, she grabbed my hand and held it. My fingers were now intertwined with hers, and I was stuck. Before I could say anything, she said, "Good morning."

"Good morning," I replied.

As she cuddled closer to my behind, she asked, "Do you want to take a shower now or do you want breakfast first?"

I didn't know. No one had ever asked me that before. Did this mean that she wanted to shower with me and that she was going to cook breakfast for me too?

"I think I'll take a shower first," I answered, with an emphasis on I'll.

"Oh, okay. Well, you can use my bathroom, I'll use the bathroom in the hall."

"No, I'll use the hall bathroom. I'm already invading your space," I said as I turned around to face her.

"You're not invading my space at all. I'd actually like to share a shower," she admitted.

I didn't know how to tell her that we shouldn't take a shower together, so I didn't. We ended up messing around in the shower just like we did in the pool house the last time. I tried to control myself, but I couldn't. My hands were all over her like an octopus. I knew that I was sober now and couldn't blame this on the alcohol.

I felt a little better after the shower. I had a small orgasm, and my head wasn't thumping as hard as it was before, but it still hurt.

"It feels like my head is about to explode."

"I'm not surprised. You became friends fast with that chick behind the bar, and she was giving you drinks on the house all night. I thought that she was trying to take you away from me."

"Take me away from her? I didn't know that I belonged to her," I said to myself before I answered, "Last night is all one big blur."

"Are you telling me that you don't remember what you did last night?"

"I think so. Wait a minute. I vaguely remember dancing on a stage and swinging from a pole. Please tell me that I didn't strip at that club last night."

"Calm down. You didn't strip, but you did dance on stage with Dawn. You remember her don't you? She is one of the most popular dancers at the club."

"Oh my God! I hope that no one recorded anything I did last night. The last thing I needed was for this to get back to Mrs. Frye. I'd lose my job for sure if these events surfaced."

"Who is Mrs. Frye?"

"She's my supervisor. She's a real pit-bull in a skirt."

"She sounds terrible."

"Honey, you don't even know half of the half."

"You can tell me. I'd like to hear about your run-ins with this wicked witch."

After we both had dried off and put on some lounge clothes, Shay started making breakfast. While she flipped our blueberry pancakes and scrambled a few eggs, I admired her tiny living quarters. The walls were bright white, but the art that hung on the walls were bold and urban. Everything blended perfectly with the denim colored couch, teal throw pillows, and khaki colored curtains. I wondered if she decorated this place herself or if someone helped her.

Over breakfast, we finished our conversation about Mrs. Frye, and I told her about my job at the high school. She couldn't believe some of the things that I had to put up with and rolled her eyes so much that I thought they were going to get stuck in the back of her head.

"Girl, I don't know how you do it. I would be in jail somewhere because I would beat the brakes off those overgrown kids. I would probably beat that principal up too."

After I had laughed, I changed the subject and asked her about her job. She had been deejaying for eight years and was one of the top female deejays in Miami. After we cleared the table and loaded the dishwasher, she showed me a photo album full of pictures of her with celebrities. I was excited to find out that Shay was a local celebrity and told her that I wanted a picture of the two of us before I left Miami.

"We can take one now if you want to."

"Nah, I look horrible," I said.

"No, you don't. You're beautiful. Come here."

As I moved in closer to her, she grabbed her phone from the coffee table and took a picture of us. After looking at the image on her cell phone, she decided that she didn't like it and moved in even closer as she held the phone up again at an angle. This time, she turned her face towards mine and kissed me on the cheek. I smiled and kissed her back as she continued to snap pictures of us. Even though we just made out in the shower, we made out again.

We rolled around on the carpet in the living room until my panties were off and her face was in between my thighs. While I panted and pushed her head deeper into my wetness, I heard my cell phone ringing from her bedroom. It could have been Trevor, but I didn't care who was calling because I was about to reach my sexual peak. As my internal temperature spiked, it felt like steam was about to come out of my ears as I called her name in ecstasy.

With my legs spread wide, Shay crawled between them and laid on top of me. After she had smiled, she gave me a quick peck on the lips and got up. I reached for my underwear and sat up. My legs felt weak, so she helped me up off of the floor. After helping me up, she didn't let my hand go, and she took me back to the bedroom.

"Lay down, let's take a nap."

I didn't know how she knew it, but I was sleepy.

"Alright," I agreed as she closed the curtains.

As the room got darker, I pulled the covers back and got comfortable on the bed.

"I'll be right back. I'm going to use the bathroom."

"Okay. I'll be right here."

Shay giggled as she went into the bathroom and closed the door. As soon as she closed the door, I reached for my phone on the floor by the bed. *"Shit, I missed Trevor's call again,"* I thought to myself as I checked my voice messages.

"Where in the hell are you? Every time I call, you never answer. I'm getting sick of this mess. I know that I told you to have a good time, but this is ridiculous. I'm not calling you again. I might not even answer the phone when you call me."

I wanted to call him, but I was tired of his wishy-washy attitude. He didn't know what he wanted, and I was sick of him. *"I'm not calling his ass back until I get back to Texas. I'll show him,"* I said to myself.

"Are you okay sweetie?" Shay asked as she climbed in the bed.

I powered my phone off and dropped it back to the floor and answered, "Yeah, I'm good."

Then I slid closer to her and put my arm around her waist.

For the next two weeks, I stayed with Shay. When she moved I moved, it's like we were connected at the hip. I went out to a few more clubs with her, but this time, I stayed away from the bar and the strippers. I had only talked to Johaly twice, and she and Leo were officially a couple. I was very happy for them, but I still didn't know exactly what was going on between Shay and me. She didn't say that I was her girlfriend, and I didn't dare ask. All I knew is that we held hands a lot and touched each other constantly.

We'd had sex over a dozen times, and we even went to the sex shop and got a few toys to use during our freak sessions. I hadn't thought about Lester at all, and I wanted to keep it that way, but when my mother called me and told me that they closed on the new house, I knew that I had to go back to the apartment and help them move.

The day of the move Shay insisted that she go with me. I didn't want her to come, but she wouldn't take no for an answer, and we got in her van and drove across town. At the apartment complex, the first person I saw when we pulled up was Lester. He was carrying a few boxes to his car. I eyeballed his strong arms as he smiled at me, but I stopped staring when Shay asked, "Where should I park?"

"Um, just back up in the space beside that guy carrying the boxes," I pointed.

She followed my instructions and got out of the van before I could open my door.

As she opened the two doors on the back of the van, I spoke to Lester and told Shay to follow me to the apartment. The walls were bare, and moving boxes were everywhere.

"It's about time you came back," Imani said.

"You must've missed me."

"A little bit. I've been playing Trouble with dad and practicing my multiplication facts. It's boring without you around."

"You better get used to me not being here, I'll be going back to Texas in a few weeks."

"Yeah, I know," she responded as she put her roller skates in a moving box.

"Oh, Imani, this is Shay. She's going to help us move today," I said as I pointed to her standing beside me.

After the two of them had exchanged greetings, we helped her take out some boxes out to the van and went back inside. As we packed up my old room, we heard my mother and Lester enter the apartment. While we took the bed apart, I tried to listen to the two of them talking through the wall, but I couldn't hear much. After she had made a few trips in and out of the apartment, she returned singing an old song called *Backstabbers* by the O'Jays. My stomach dropped when her voice got closer to my room, and I instantly thought that she knew about what Lester and I had done.

I froze as she pushed the door open and said, "Hey baby. We're about to take the first load of stuff over to the new house in a few minutes. Do you think I can put the coffee table in your friend's van?" Before I could answer, Shay said, "Sure, this mattress should be able to fit too. Just give us a few more seconds and we'll be out there." "Alright," Mom said as she disappeared without closing the door to the room.

I took a deep breath because I thought that the shit was about to hit the fan. I knew that Lester said he wouldn't tell her, and I believed him, but I couldn't help feeling guilty. While I was in mid thought, Shay broke the silence and asked, "What's wrong?" "Oh, nothing. I'm fine, let's get this mattress out of here, so we can get the first load of stuff to the new house."

After we put the mattress and box spring in the back of the van, Lester slid the coffee table in, along with a few more items and shut the doors. "I think that we're ready to make our first drop," he said as he walked to the passenger side of the van. I nodded my head and rolled up the window, then he got into his car with Mom and Imani and started the engine.

Shay followed Lester a few blocks before he put on his signal and turned into a concrete driveway. This place looked very familiar to me; then I remembered passing by this house on the way to the nail spa. The only thing that was missing was the for sale sign in the yard. The cream-colored stucco house had a reddish orange tile roof with dark brown shutters. There was a small porch attached to the front of the house and an attached carport. The outside of the house looked beautiful, and I couldn't wait to see how the inside looked.

I just realized how excited I was when my mother jumped out of Lester's car and held up the keys to the new house. I felt like a child all over again as I bum-rushed her and ran to the front door to unlock it. The paint, tile, cabinets, and layout was perfect. Of course, she had purchased a three bedroom house. She had to have that extra bedroom. The rooms were much bigger than the apartment, and there was a backyard with a fence and storage shed. After I ran from room to room, I sat in the empty soaker tub and kicked my feet up on the end of it.

"That extra bedroom is for you," Mom said as she entered the master bath and sat on the edge of the tub.

"Are you serious?"

"Yeah. I'm dead serious. Since Trevor isn't sure of what he wants to do, I wanted to get a place big enough if you decided to move back. I hate the thought of you living in Texas with no family."

"Mom, that is so sweet, but I'll continue to live in Texas with or without Trevor. I make enough money to support myself; I'll be okay."

"Well, there is an extra room here if you ever decide to come back."

Before she helped me out of the tub, we shared a hug and went outside to help bring in the first load of boxes. As we unloaded the vehicles, Imani started putting things where they belonged. She started in the kitchen first and put the dishes away. When we were finished unloading everything, we all got back in the cars and went back to the apartment complex to get the rest of the boxes and furniture.

After our third trip to the new house, Lester let Imani stay so she could start unpacking her bedroom and the hall bathroom. Every time we came back to drop off more boxes, it looked more like a home. Imani was doing an excellent job unpacking and organizing things. I wished that she could go back to Texas with me to keep my apartment clean and tidy.

Three trips later we were ready to load up one final time, and I was glad because in between packing up the linen closet, Shay stole kisses from my lips and I had gotten very aroused. Since there were only a few boxes, Lester and Mom helped fill the van up and left to get a few more things for the new house. After Shay and I double checked the apartment one final time we locked the door and headed to the new house.

As soon as we pulled into the driveway, Shay's phone rang. After she had put the van in park, I let her have some privacy and went inside to get Imani to help me unload the van. After unlocking the front door, I heard music playing. When I called Imani, she didn't answer. I knew that she had to be here because her shoes were by the front door.

My heart dropped after I called for her again and she didn't answer. I walked quickly down the hallway only to be slapped in the face by the strong smell of marijuana. Just then I heard a cough come from the bathroom, and I twisted the knob. The door was locked, but it wasn't shut all the way, so after I pushed it, it came open.

I don't know who was more surprised, Imani or me.

"Why does it smell like marijuana smoke in here?"

"I don't smell anything," she said as smoke came out of her mouth.

"You little brat, I know you're not in this house smoking. Where did you get that weed from?"

"From my friend, please don't tell. I'll flush it down the toilet now."

"Give me that," I yelled as I snatched the small baggie from Imani. "Do you have any idea how much trouble you can get into with this?"

"No, I wasn't planning on getting caught with it."

"Girl, what in the hell is wrong with you? Your dad would kill you if he caught you with this, don't you know that this is illegal? You can go to jail for having this. Do you want to go to jail?"

Before I could say anything else, Imani broke out into sobs, "No, I just wanted to be cool. My friends said that this stuff would make me feel better about myself."

"This shit ain't going to make you feel like nothing. After you smoke that crap all you'll feel like doing is being lazy and eating all the food you can get your hands on. What in the hell are you stressed out about? You're only twelve."

"I don't have any boobs yet. All the other girls have boobs. I want some too."

"If I don't know anything else. I know for sure that smoking weed isn't going to make your boobs grow. If you want, I can take you to the mall and shop for a few padded bras before I go back home. You'll have to remember to wear your padded bras every day because if you don't, the boys will notice."

After not getting any kind of response from Imani, I looked at her with a serious face and then added, "But, if you want to walk around with yellow teeth and stinky breath, go ahead. You'll never get a boyfriend smelling like an ashtray."

I hoped that the reverse psychology would work on her as I walked slowly out of the bathroom. Just as I stepped over the threshold, she said, "When can you take me to the mall?"

"Sometime this week."

"Alright, you promise?" She asked as she tossed the small blunt into the toilet. After I had turned away from her, I smiled and said, "Yeah, I promise. Don't forget to flush the toilet, let the window up, turn on the fan, spray some air freshener, take a shower, and brush your teeth. Our parents will be back soon, and you don't want it to smell like weed in here."

As I walked down the hall, I heard Imani close the bathroom door, spray a half can of air freshener, flush the toilet, and turn the shower on. I shook my head and pushed the baggie of weed down in my pocket before I yelled, "Turn the fan on." As soon as I got the last word out of my mouth, I heard the fan come on.

When I got back outside Shay was still on the phone. I wondered who she was talking to as I opened one of the back doors of the van and reached inside to grab a box. I took two boxes inside before she got off the phone and helped me. As soon as she stepped in the house, she said, "It smells like weed in here. It didn't smell like this the last time. If it did, I didn't notice." Just then Imani came out of the bathroom and headed to her room.

12

Puff Puff Pass

Shay and I ended up staying with Imani until my mother and Lester returned from the store. I was trying to hook the cable up to the back of the television when I heard a horn blow. Then we all put our shoes on and went outside to help bring in the bags from Wal-Mart, Big Lots, and Food Lion. Just when we thought that we had everything put away, we had more stuff to put up. While Shay bent down to put food in the pantry, Lester watched her rear end with hungry eyes.

I was surprised that no one else noticed. I guess they were too busy putting the groceries up. By the time we left, we were so tired that we only went to Shay's house and got into bed. Neither one of said anything about showering or moved a muscle after we got into bed. My body was so sore from carrying boxes all day that I almost forgot that I had a baggie of weed in my back pocket.

Without saying a word about the weed, I pulled it out and held it up in the air.

"Look what Imani gave me today."

As Shay looked over in my direction, she said, "What's that? I hope that's not what I think it is."

"Yes, ma'am. That's what it is."

"What in the hell is Imani doing with a bag of marijuana and where did she get it from?"

"She said that she got it from one of her friends. I think the one that Lester let her finally stay the night with."

"Damn, that's a shame. So did she just give it to you out of the blue?"

"No, I caught her smoking it in the bathroom and snatched the baggie out of her hand."

"I knew that it smelled like weed when I walked in the house this afternoon."

"Yeah. She had a blunt and everything. She flushed it down the toilet after I used some reverse psychology on her."

"Oh Really? What are you going to do with that?" She said as she eyeballed the baggie.

"I was going to see if you wanted it."

"Yeah. I'll smoke it. Do you want to smoke it with me?"

I knew that I should have said no, but I said yes. I hadn't smoked weed since my college days and missed the feeling of total relaxation that it gave me.

"I need to get a cigar. I'm going to the corner store. Do you want to ride with me?"

"Nope," I answered.

"Okay, I'll be back in a few minutes."

Before Shay rolled out of the bed, she gave me a kiss on the cheek and grabbed her keys off of the nightstand. After she slid her small feet into her sneakers, she left the bedroom, and I heard the front door open and close. When the engine of her van started, I got up and got my phone from my purse. No one had called me today, and I wondered how Mark was doing. Without thinking, I dialed his number and waited to hear his voice answer the phone. I was a bit disappointed when he didn't answer but figured that he was working and left him a message.

Since I was up, I went to my suitcase, picked out a pair of pajamas, and started the shower. I didn't feel like bathing, but I had to wash the sweat from my body, and I knew that the hot water would help relieve the soreness in my muscles. In the shower, I thought about Lester's big chocolate cock. I wanted to ride him again and imagined how good it would feel. I squeezed my nipples and thought of how good it felt when he nibbled at them.

The shower almost pushed me over the edge, but I didn't climax because I heard the front door open and close again. I cut my playtime short and finished showering because I knew that Shay was back. Just as I rinsed the remainder of suds down the drain, I heard her say, "I'm back baby." After I dried off, I didn't bother putting on any clothes and sauntered into the room naked. I carried my pajamas in one hand and a bottle of lotion in the other.

"You smell good," she said as she watched me throw my pajamas back in my suitcase and pulled the covers back on her bed.

"I feel like a million bucks."

"I think I can make you feel better than a million bucks."

"We'll see about that," I replied with a smirk.

While I sat on the edge of the bed and massaged lotion onto my damp skin, Shay busted a cigar open, removed the tobacco, and replaced it with the weed that Imani had given me. While she rolled and saturated the blunt with saliva, I propped a few pillows up behind my back. There was nothing on television, so I left it on the weather channel. I already knew that it was going to be hot as hell, but there was some nice jazz playing in the background, so I left it there.

"You want to hit this bad boy first?" She asked as she lit the end of the blunt.

"Nah, you go first. You did all the hard work. You deserve the first puff."

Without saying another word she took my advice and put the blunt to her lips. She puffed a few times and then handed it to me. Before I put it to my lips, the voice in my head said, *"Are you sure that you want to do this? The last thing you need to do is fail a drug test at work. You can't afford to lose your job right now with your relationship still in limbo with Trevor. Don't do it."*

Before the voice could utter another word, I took my first puff and inhaled. My throat felt like it caught on fire as I choked and gagged. "I need some water," I said while I coughed like someone who had tuberculosis. Shay scrambled for a glass in the nearby kitchen and returned quickly. After she handed the glass to me, I took a big gulp and looked at her. Then we both burst out laughing as she took the blunt from me and took a smooth puff before she said, "This is how you're supposed to do it." Then she passed the blunt back to me.

"Okay," I replied as I set the glass of water on the nightstand and took my second puff. This time, I didn't choke. After passing the blunt back and forth for another ten minutes or so, the feeling of calm and relaxation came over me. When Shay left to take a shower, I finished smoking the blunt alone and stared at the row of one hundred degree temperature readings on the television screen. At the moment I wasn't worried about work or Trevor, all I knew is that I was high.

I don't know how long Shay was in the shower, but when she came out, she snatched the covers off of me and pulled me by my feet to the foot of the bed. With my legs wide open and her head buried between my thighs, I called out to her over and over again. While she kissed my most private parts, I enjoyed each and every solitary lick. When I thought she was going to come up for air, she surprised me by sucking on the top of my clitoris. Just as I was about to climax, she inserted a few fingers inside of me and slowly moved them in and out. I gave in and had an orgasm that was from out of this world. I shivered as my body temperature rose a few degrees and sweat rolled from my brow.

I felt as if I didn't have any energy until she straddled me and I caressed her firm behind. I didn't know what was about to happen next, so I just went with the flow until she said, "I want you to ride my face."

"What?"

"You heard me. I want you to sit on my face."

I sat on Trevor's face plenty of times, but this was different. I'd never sat on a girl's face before.

"No, let me please you," I said as I tried to push her off of me.

"No, tonight is all about you."

With no more ifs, ands, or buts, I did as she said. I never knew that sex could be so good without a real live penis. After I rode her face, she pulled out a few sex toys that we got from the adult store, and she spent the rest of the night pleasuring me. I felt like a queen and knew that I would remember this night for the rest of my life. Nothing that Trevor, Lester, or Manny ever did felt this good and I was secretly wondering if Shay and I were girlfriends.

The very next day, I woke up with a nasty taste in my mouth and wished that I didn't smoke that blunt. Now that my high was gone, I was officially a wreck. All I could think about was getting a drug test at school and losing my job. When I mentioned losing my job to Shay, she brushed it off and asked, "Have they ever given you a drug test before?"

"No," I answered with concern in my voice.

"Well, what makes you think that you're going to get a drug test then? Stop thinking negative thoughts."

"I don't know. I wish that I wouldn't have smoked that shit last night."

"Don't fret; there's this stuff that you can take to get it out of your system in a few days. They sell it at the vitamin shop. We can get you some later today."

"Are you sure that it will work?"

"Yes. I'm sure."

"How sure are you?"

"About ninety percent," she said with a laugh.

"That's not funny."

"Hey, if you do get fired, you can come and live with me."

I didn't know how to respond to that, so I only said, "That shit at the vitamin shop better work."

"It will. Now stop worrying and get in the kitchen and cook me something to eat. As good as I freaked you last night, I shouldn't have to say anything about breakfast. I should already be eating."

"Oh, I got something that you can eat," I laughed as I hit her with a pillow and went to the bathroom to wash up.

After I was finished in the bathroom, I went straight to the kitchen and started cooking for my girlfriend or friend girl. Whichever you want to call it. Then I thought about how life would be living here in Miami with Shay. This summer fling that we were having was all fun, but I couldn't see myself in a relationship with a woman. No matter how hard I tried, I couldn't see it. Whatever happened in Miami, was going to stay in Miami. Just like they say about Vegas.

Later that night, I drank the drug-be-gone concoction from the vitamin shop while Shay got ready for work. She begged me to go with her, but I feared that I wouldn't be able to control myself and decided to sit this one out. Don't get me wrong. I was down for a good time, but I had been drinking like a fish since I got to Miami and smoking that weed last night made me realize that I was going overboard. Since I wasn't going out to party tonight, I planned on spending some time with Imani.

Shay looked sexy in her black cotton catsuit and black boots that had lots of chains and buckles hanging from them. I wondered how I would look if I wore something like that.

"I'd never worn black nail polish before or a catsuit," I thought as I looked at my nails.

"Why are you so quiet tonight?" She asked.

"No reason, I'm just thinking. You know, it'll be time for me to go back home soon. This vacation is flying by."

"Time flies when you're having fun."

"It sure does."

"So are you sure that you don't want to go to the club with me tonight? You can stay upstairs with me near the deejay booth."

"Nah, I'm going to hang out with Imani. Can you drop me off on your way to the club?"

"I sure can. Do you want me to pick you up on my way back home?"

I thought long and hard before I answered this question.

"Nah, I'm going to stay the night with Imani. I haven't been spending any time with her lately, and I feel like I need to talk to her some more about this whole smoking marijuana thing."

"Oh, yeah that's right. It's going to be lonely sleeping without you tonight."

"I'll be back tomorrow. You just make sure that you don't bring any of those dancers home tonight."

"I'd never do that," Shay said and then added, "Now give me some sugar."

After swapping spit with Shay, I got up and collected a few of my things to take over to the new house. When my bag was packed, I cut the light off in the bedroom and waited for Shay to make us both a drink before we headed out the door. Before I buckled up in the van, I took my cell phone out of my purse and dialed my mother's cell phone number. When she answered, I asked, "Are you home?" "Yeah, are you coming over?" "Yes ma'am, I am. I was just making sure that someone was home." "We're all here, I'm cooking now because I may go to the bingo hall, but Lester and Imani will be here."

My heart dropped when I learned that Lester and I may be alone again tonight. I hoped I could control myself as Shay pulled out of the driveway. I stayed silent and didn't say a word until we were almost to my mother's place.

"Did you finish your drink yet?" I asked her.

"Nope, I haven't drunk any of it."

"Can I have it?"

"Sure, I can get another one when I get to the club."

"Are you okay?"

"I'm good," I responded after I downed the drink in three gulps and looked out of the window.

When we pulled in front of my mother's house, I reached for the door handle. "Wait, I'd like a kiss before you go. I'm not going to see you until tomorrow," she said. Before I leaned over to give her a goodbye kiss, I looked around to see if anyone was watching. It was almost dusk, and there was no one in sight, so I gave her a kiss. The last thing I needed was for Mom, Lester, or Imani to see us kissing. I was grown, and I didn't owe any explanations to anyone, but I wasn't ready for my family to know that I was bisexual.

13

Getting Lucky

Before I could knock on the door, Lester opened it and let me inside. He had a stupid looking grin on his face, and I hoped that he hadn't seen us kissing in the van. "It's good to see you," he said as he looked me up and down. "I just saw you yesterday," I replied as I crossed the threshold. After he had winked his eye, he said, "I know."

Just then my mother yelled from the kitchen, "Summer, is that you?"

"Yes, Mom. It's me."

"Taste this lemonade that Imani made. It's delicious; I told her that she needs to set up a lemonade stand."

"Where is Imani anyway?" I asked as I looked around.

"She's taking a bath in the soaker tub in my room. She should be out in a few minutes. She's been in there for over an hour. I hope she hasn't used all the hot water," Lester answered while walking closely behind me.

Before I sat down at the table, I rinsed my hands off and grabbed a glass out of the cabinet. After filling it with crushed ice from the new refrigerator, I poured it full of lemonade. Just as I was about to take a sip, Lester asked me to fix him some too. "Here you can have this one," I said as I handed him the glass and fixed myself another one.

"Damn, this is good baby."

I immediately froze because I thought that Lester was talking to me. When I turned around to look, he was looking in my mother's direction. My heart thumped wildly as I poured another glass of lemonade and sat down across from him at the table. After I had taken a deep breath, I took a sip and couldn't stop drinking. Lester and Mom were right. This sweet and sour concoction was good. I drank it straight down and poured a refill as Imani entered the kitchen.

"Hey, Summer. I didn't know that you were here."

"Yeah, I came to spend some time with you. My vacation is winding down, and I'll be going home soon. Maybe we can go to the mall tomorrow or at least hang out by the pool at Johaly's."

"That sounds like fun, but I'm going skating tonight with one of my friends. Her mom should be here any minute to pick me up. The place opens at eight."

"Oh, well I guess I'll go back to Shay's then."

"No, please stay. I will be back by eleven. We can watch a movie or even play a board game with Dad like we did the last time."

I hesitated before I answered, "Okay. I'll find something to do around here while you're gone."

"Dammit, this meant that Lester and I were going to be alone tonight for at least a few hours," I thought as my mother put a piping hot plate of fried chicken, candy yams, rice, gravy, and butter beans down in front of me. While I watched the steam rise from my plate, I said a silent prayer and asked for the ability to resist Lester.

Mom and Imani carried on a conversation about her lemonade while I tried to focus on my prayer. After a minute of staring at my food, I grabbed my fork and began eating. Lester ate his food quietly as Imani gobbled her food up quickly.

"I wish you would slow down. You're going to burn your mouth," my mom said.

"I can't help it. I'm hungry, and my ride will be here any minute."

Just then, a horn sounded from outside, and Imani scrambled to her feet, but not before shoving another forkful of food into her mouth.

"That's my ride. Summer, I'll see you when I get back. Don't leave," she said as she spoke with greasy lips and a mouth full of food.

"I'll walk you outside," Lester announced as he got up from the table.

When they both left the kitchen, my mother asked me if I wanted to go to the bingo hall with her tonight. After turning her down all the time, I decided to take her up on her offer. Maybe I could win some money this evening; God knows I needed some extra cash after agreeing to take Imani to the mall.

"Alright Mom. I'll go."

"Really?"

"Yeah. I'm feeling lucky. Maybe I can win big like you did."

"The jackpot is back up to five thousand dollars. Wouldn't that make a great addition to your bank account?"

"Yes, it would."

"As soon as I'm finished eating we can go."

"Go where?" Lester asked as he entered the kitchen.

"Oh, Summer finally agreed to go to the bingo hall with me."

The look on Lester's face was a little unclear when he heard the news about being left home alone until he opened his mouth.

"You can't hang with your mom all night. I bet you'll be back before she will," he said with a smirk.

"I guess we'll have to see because I'm going to press my luck tonight."

"Lester you can come too," my mother suggested.

"Nah, I'll stick around the house. I might be able to find a good movie on television, plus someone needs to be here when Imani gets back from the skating rink."

Before we left the house, my mother grabbed her lucky rabbit's foot and a new box of ink daubers. She bent down and gave Lester a kiss right before we walked out the door. I didn't see her kiss him. I only heard the wet sound that their lips made when they came in contact with each other, and it made my skin crawl.

When I got into Lester's Cadillac, the first thing I did was buckled up because my mother drove like a race car driver. I didn't know that the bingo hall was so far away. It took us over twenty minutes to get there. We passed by three different bingo halls before we reached our destination. I made sure that mom had put the car in park before I took my seat belt off. I never had whiplash before, but it felt like I had a bad case of it. My neck and shoulders were hurting because of the sudden stops and fast turns that my mother made through the city. I was going to drive back because I couldn't handle another twenty minutes of being jerked around.

The inside of the bingo hall was painted bright white, and the fluorescent bulbs hummed and flickered as we entered the building. I never imagined seeing almost one hundred tables lined up with people sitting at each one. Before we found a table near the caller, we purchased our bingo cards and two bottles of water.

While people around us chatted and ate hot dogs, popcorn, and nachos we walked towards the front of the room. Mom sat down beside a lady and introduced us.

"Bessie this is my one and only baby girl."

"Nice to meet you," we both said at the same time.

Bessie's hair was silver. She didn't look old, but she had a head full of silver hair. *"Maybe it's a wig,"* I thought as I reached into the box of ink daubers. While my mother spread her cards out, she talked and bragged about the new house. Bessie smiled as she complimented me on the color of my eyes and took a sip of her Pepsi.

"Where is my lucky rabbit's foot?" Mom asked.

"I think that you put it in your purse. Oh no, here it is. It's in the bag with the daubers."

I pulled the blue rabbit's foot out and sat it on the table along with a hot pink bingo dauber.

Not too long after we were settled at the table, a man's voice came over the intercom, and everyone stopped talking. The man gave the rules and regulations of the games, then he rang a bell and wished everyone good luck. As the man called out letter and number combinations, I filled one of my bingo cards quickly and yelled "BINGO."

I think I startled my mother because she jumped when I yelled. After I heard a bunch of sighs come from the table next to us, I rolled my eyes and held my card up in the air. Then an older white woman came to check my card. I held my breath as she called out my numbers to the man that was sitting on the platform. "Yep, she's a winner," the man said. I had two cards left and the woman told me to take it to the desk near the front of the building to claim my prize.

After I had won two hundred dollars, I put the check in my pocket and went back to the table with my mother and Bessie. I had two cards left and I was ready to win again. After an hour had passed and I hadn't won anything else, I was ready to go. Lester was right. We hadn't been here that long, and my back was starting to hurt from sitting in the beige metal folding chairs. My mother hadn't won anything yet, and she watched her ten cards cautiously as I told her that I was going to call a cab to take me back to the house.

"Okay, baby."

"What am I supposed to do with these cards?"

"Give them to me. I'll play them for you, and if you win, I'll give you the money."

"Okay. That sounds good," I said.

"You can drive Lester's car back. If you take a cab, you'll end up spending most of your winnings on the ride."

"Are you sure, how are you going to get home?"

"I'll get Bessie to give me a ride. Now get out of here you're interfering with my game."

"Okay. I'll drive Lester's car. I'll see you when you get home. Good luck," I said as I reached into her purse and got the keys.

On the way home, Trevor crossed my mind, and I called him. I didn't get an answer. I wasn't surprised, so I called Mark and told him about the new house and the adventures with my mom at the bingo hall. He confessed that he missed me terribly and couldn't wait until I got back to Texas. I told him that I missed him too and promised to give him a call tomorrow after I figured out what I was going to do with Imani.

When I pulled up in the yard, I put the car in park and grabbed my purse before I got out. To my surprise, Lester was waiting on me at the door just like he was earlier. As soon as I walked inside of the house, I called out for Imani, and she didn't answer.

"Where is Imani? Is she asleep?"

"No. I let her stay the night with her friend. She called back to talk to you, and I told her that you went to the bingo hall with your mother. After she heard the news, she asked if she could stay with her friend and I told her yes. She just left with a duffle bag full of clothes a few minutes before you pulled up."

"Really?" I said with a bit of sarcasm in my voice.

"Yes, it looks like it's just going to be me and you until your mother gets back from the bingo hall," he said with a devilish smile.

"Look, I know what you're thinking."

"You do?" He asked as he moved in a little closer.

"Yeah, and we don't need to do this again."

"You know what. You need to make your mind up. One day you don't want me, then the next day you do want me. You can't toy with an old man's emotions like that."

"I'm sorry Lester, it never should've gone this far."

"You damn right. It should never have gone this far. I can't get your sweet ass off my mind. Do you know how long it's been since I had some nice tight stuff like yours?"

"No."

"It's been about twenty years or so. Come on. Just let me taste you tonight. Please."

"No, it's not right."

"Shit. I knew you were going to flake up on me. I knew that this was too good to be true."

"Don't be mad. Even you said that we shouldn't do it again."

"That was before you seduced me with that hot box that you got between your legs."

I stood with my arms folded and listened to him talk. As his mouth moved, I tuned him out and stared at his mustache.

"I don't have time for that yapping," I said as I started to walk away from him.

"You don't have time for my yapping? Well, what about this? Do you have time for this?" He asked as he withdrew his ding-a-ling out of his pajamas.

After I took a long look. I cleared my throat before I replied, "Now, why would you do a thing like that for?"

"I knew you couldn't resist this big black cock."

"Let me freshen up a bit and I'll be back in a jiffy."

"Alright, we'll be waiting for you," he said as he stroked himself and then added, "Bring a towel when you come back, you don't want the couch cushion to get wet again."

Without going to my room to get my pajamas, I went into the bathroom in the hallway and started the shower. After I had stripped, I stepped in and got fresh and clean. Not even ten minutes later I was finished and wrapped in a towel. Just as I headed out the bathroom, I realized that I needed some lotion or body oil because my skin felt dry.

After I opened up the cabinet, I saw a bottle of Suave lotion and reached in to grab it when I noticed a small blunt towards the back of the cabinet. *"That little heffa,"* I thought to myself as I picked it up and put it on top of the counter. "Could there be more weed in the cabinet?" I whispered as I moved bottles of alcohol, shampoo, tissue, conditioner, and maxi pads around. I didn't see any weed, and I thanked God as I put everything back like it was when I found it, including the blunt. "I'll talk to her little ass tomorrow," I said as I squirted some lotion into my palms.

As I opened the bathroom door, I called for Lester, and he said, "I hope you're ready." Yeah, I'm ready I replied as I walked over and sat on his lap. He had put his penis back into his pajamas, but he was still excited. I rested one of my legs against it while he started kissing my neck and nibbling on my ears. Then one of his hands made its way between my legs, and he began to stimulate my clitoris. He did this for a few minutes before he moved me off of his lap and fell onto his knees.

While he knelt down in front of me, I spread the towel out and sat with my legs pinned up against my chest. The position was a little uncomfortable, but I knew that I wouldn't mind after Lester started to please me. His mustache tickled my fancy as he lowered his face and took his first lick. A tingle ran up my spine as I relaxed and closed my eyes. I was somewhere over the rainbow when I heard a door shut and opened my eyes.

My heart sank to my toes when I heard my mom say, "Alright, Bessie. Thanks for the ride."

Then I saw a set of headlights flash across the window. "Oh my God. Mom is home," I whispered as I jumped up and snatched the towel off the couch. I ran towards my bedroom as she unlocked the front door.

In my room, I threw the towel in my closet and stepped in a pair of jogging pants that were folded near the foot of my bed. While I frantically searched for a shirt, I heard my mother say, "Lester what on earth are you doing on the floor?" After a brief pause, he answered, "I'm looking for the remote." "It's right there on the coffee table. If it were a snake it would have bitten you," she giggled and then asked, "Where's Summer? Her card hit again after she left." "I think that she's in her room."

When I heard footsteps getting closer to my room, I slid on a wrinkled t-shirt and hopped on the bed with my phone. I pretended that I was sending a text message as she knocked once and let herself in. "Oh hey Mom, you're back early tonight?" I said as I nervously sat up. "Yeah, Bessie had to go home because her husband locked himself out of the house again. I think the old fart is getting a touch of Alzheimer's. Anyway, your bingo card hit four corners right before we left." "For real?" "Yes, ma'am, here you go," she said as she handed me a wad of cash and left.

After separating the bills, I counted a little more than four hundred dollars. I never knew that I could win so much money playing bingo, and I was sorry that I'd never gone with her to play bingo before. As a matter of fact, I was going to look into finding a bingo hall when I got back to Texas. I had pretty good luck here in Miami, and I hoped that it would follow me back home.

Before I turned the lamp on my nightstand off, I called Shay, but she was still working. She answered the phone, but all I could hear was loud music. I could barely make out what she said, but I heard her say, "I love you" loud and clear before she hung up. Damn, what did I get myself into with her? I honestly didn't know if I loved her or not, but I knew that I loved the way that she makes me feel.

14

Three's a Crowd

That night I didn't sleep well at all because I heard my mother and Lester having sex. I guess his engine was still tuned-up from what we had done on the couch before she disturbed our groove. After tossing and turning for a few hours, I got up and slipped a robe on over my night shirt. The door to my bedroom creaked open as I went across the hallway to use the bathroom. On my way out, I got a sudden urge for a cup of coffee and made a detour to the kitchen.

As I walked through the living room, I looked at the couch and the remote sitting on the coffee table, and my stomach began to hurt. I couldn't believe that Lester and I nearly got caught. I almost jumped out of my skin when I turned the corner and saw him sitting at the kitchen table with the lights off.

"Good morning."

"Good morning," I replied.

"What are you doing up so early?"

"I couldn't sleep."

"Neither could I," I said as I opened the cabinet above the coffee maker and added, "Where's Mom? Is she still asleep?"

"No, she went to the indoor flea market in the shopping plaza around the corner. She said that the early bird gets the worm."

I giggled before I reached in the bread box to get a bagel and replied, "Ain't that the truth."

"You can get this worm right now if you want to." He said as he pointed to his penis under the table.

"Are you crazy? After what happened last night, we can't take any more chances."

"You're right. That was crazy. I couldn't even get up off of my knees in time."

"What did mom say when she saw your erection?"

"She didn't see it. After she had left your room, she went into our room and took a shower. By the time she came out my erection had subsided. But she was frisky, so we ended up having sex."

"I know, I heard the moans coming from down the hallway. That's one of the reasons why I couldn't sleep."

After I poured us each a cup of coffee and spread some cream cheese on my bagel, I joined him at the table. As soon as I took my first bite, Lester asked, "Do you think that you can make an old man's dream come true?"

"If the price is right, I may be able to."

"That girl that you brought over here with the van. She helped us move."

"Yeah, yeah. What about her?" I asked in a hurry.

"I watched the two of you interacting with each other when you thought nobody was watching."

"And..."

"Well, are y'all bumping and grinding?"

"If you must know. Yes, we are. She's my brown sugar."

"Do you think that we could arrange a threesome? Or maybe I could just watch you guys get it on?"

"I'll see what I can do, but only if you promise that we get a little one on one action before I leave, but we can't do it here at the house."

"That sounds like a plan. I can't wait to feel that sweet mouth of yours again. Your mother doesn't like oral sex."

"I didn't need to know that," I dryly said as I took a sip of my coffee.

"Oh, sorry."

After talking to him about a possible threesome, I put some clothes on and left. Instead of calling Shay to pick me up, I walked to her house. It took me almost forty minutes, but I didn't care, I had to clear my head. While I walked, I thought of ways that I could bring up the threesome conversation to Shay. I wrecked my brain for the entire walk and still didn't know how I would ask her.

As I approached Shay's cute little house, I walked across the grass and onto the porch. After I rang the doorbell twice. I didn't get an answer and knocked on the window. After waiting a few more minutes, she opened the door wrapped in a sheet and let me in.

"Hey, baby. I thought that you were going to call me when you wanted me to pick you up from your moms."

"Yeah, that's what I planned on doing, but I felt like walking, so here I am."

"Make yourself at home. I'm going to take a shower. I just got home two hours ago. Things got crazy at the club last night."

"What?"

"Yeah, it was some ballers in the club. They made it rain all over the place. One of the guys tipped me a thousand dollars after he said that I was cute, and my mixing skills were dope. Can you believe that?"

"That is unbelievable. I guess we both had a streak of good luck last night. Two of my bingo cards hit, and I won some cash."

"That's great. I guess we both got lucky last night."

For the remainder of the day, I couldn't stop thinking about the threesome that Lester requested. After Shay had showered, she ended up falling asleep on the couch with her head in my lap. I tried to watch television while she caught up on her beauty rest until Imani called me. She wanted to know if I was coming back over and I said no. After she sucked her teeth and hung up the phone, I was tempted to call her back and ask her about the blunt that I found in the bathroom cabinet.

I didn't know what was going on with that child, but I was going to find out. Not too long after I sent Mark and Trevor text messages,

Shay woke up with a smile and told me to get dressed. After I asked her where we were going, she said that it was some place nice and to dress up. As I showered, I wondered what she had up her sleeve.

While we both got dolled up, we hardly said anything to each other as one of her mixed CD's played. I sang to the songs inside of my head as Ryan Leslie, B.O.B, and John Legend sang about love and beautiful girls. I had to remember to get a copy of this CD before my vacation was over, because it made me feel so relaxed. I applied some eyeshadow to the lids of my eyes as Shay zipped the zipper on her tan leather wedges and we both were ready.

After she had locked the door, we walked to the van and she opened the passenger door for me. *"This was a first,"* I thought while I buckled up and watched her walk around to the driver's side. When she climbed in, she looked over and winked at me before she started the engine. Like always the music pumped through the speakers, this time, she sang out loud. I only looked out the window and wondered where we were going.

Shay drove for thirty minutes or so before we pulled in front of a very fancy steakhouse. A valet driver approached the van, and she handed him a twenty dollar bill. Then she got out, and I did too. While she waited for me at the door, I watched the valet driver park the van a few yards away. After he had got out the van, he made his way back to a podium type stand and put a tag on the keys. Before he hung the keys on a set of hooks, he grabbed a piece of paper with a series of numbers on it and tore the perforated part off.

When he handed it to me, he said, "You'll need this when you come back to get your vehicle."

"Oh okay," I answered as Shay took me by the hand and the other valet guy opened the door of the restaurant for us.

While Shay gave the woman behind the counter her information for the reservations, I wondered if this was a date. The groups of people that were waiting in the lobby watched every move that we made while she talked to the hostess. I was going to say something to the gawkers, but I didn't have a chance to because the hostess took us to a candlelit booth right away.

Before we sat down, Shay kissed me on the cheek and let my hand go. I blushed a little because a new group of eyeballs was watching us now. As we settled in the booth, I couldn't contain myself any longer and blurted, "Is this a date?"

"This can be whatever you want it to be," she replied without looking up from her menu.

I didn't know what to say as I looked down at the menu and noticed how expensive this place was. *"Damn, this had to be a date,"* I thought before I cautiously placed my order when the waiter arrived. We dined on steak, grilled shrimp, and creamed spinach. I felt a little tipsy as I ordered my third glass of wine and asked her about her sex life.

"Can I ask you a personal question?"

"Sure, you can ask me anything."

After I had leaned a little closer, I asked in a whisper, "Have you ever been with a man?"

"Of course, I have. Only two, though."

"How do you feel about me? Well, about what we have going on?"

"Obviously, I like you. I actually love you. I've never been in this type of situation before. I mean I've kissed girls, but I've never gone this far with one. Working at strip clubs a lot of the dancers hit on me. One even tried to go down on me in the deejay booth one night while I was packing my equipment up."

Before I could catch myself, my emotions came alive, and I felt a little jealous and said, "Shay, I love you too. I mean, I care about you. And when did this stripper try to go down on you?"

After she had let out a laugh, she said, "Calm down. That happened before I met you and I know that you love me. I can tell by the way you touch me."

As much as we talked that night, I still didn't allow myself to ask her about the threesome. Since she claimed that she loved me, I didn't want to do anything to make her feelings change towards me, so I didn't mention it at all.

A few days went by before Lester called me. Of course, I knew what he wanted and why he was calling. He was starting to get on my nerves. Since I was tired of hearing about the threesome, I decided that the next time he asked I was going to lie and tell him that Shay said no. Besides, I didn't want them to be sneaking around after I left.

That same evening I was on the phone catching up with Mark and Lester beeped in. I took a deep breath and tried not to get an attitude as I switched lines and answered the call.

"Hey, Summer. Did you ask her yet?"

"Yeah, she said no to both the threesome and letting you watch us," I lied.

"I knew that this was too good to be true. I've been dreaming about this for the past week, and now it's not going to happen."

"Hold on. I think that I can make this work, you may be able to watch us from the closet, but you have to be quiet, and you can't record us."

"Record y'all? What kind of pervert do you think I am?"

"I don't know. Look I'm sorry. I shouldn't have said that."

"Look baby girl, I'm interested in watching from the closet, but I'm not sure if I can handle that. I may want to come out and join you guys."

"I already told you that she said no. If I let you watch from the closet, Shay won't even know that you're in there."

"How in the hell am I supposed to be quiet? When I see the two of you ladies going down on each other, I'll probably lose my mind and start howling like a wolf at a full moon."

"If you want to watch, you've got to be able to control yourself. I can set up a small area in the closet with a towel and some lube while Shay and I handle our business. I'll make sure I play some music too, just in case you can't control yourself and want to shout out or something."

"Sounds like music to my ears, let me know when and where and I'll be there."

"Alright. It will be within the next few days."

"The sooner, the better," he replied before he hung up.

I could tell that he was smiling through the phone as I clicked back over and finished my conversation with Mark.

For the next two nights, I tossed and turned thinking about how I could get Lester into Shay's house. He couldn't park his long Cadillac in the driveway or down the street, and if he left his car at home and walked here, my mother would wonder why he'd left his car. With all the neighborhood watch signs that were posted in Shay's neighborhood, I knew that he couldn't just walk up to her house in the middle of the night without someone possibly seeing him and calling the cops.

I didn't have the extra money to get a hotel room, even though I won the money at bingo the other night, I still had to take Imani shopping for padded bras, and I hadn't heard a thing from Trevor. I had to conserve my money just in case Trevor didn't come around when I got back to Texas, so I thought long and hard until the perfect scenario came to mind.

We were going to have to get a hotel. I figured that it would be less risky if we went to a hotel. I would make Lester pay for the room. I'd make sure that he paid in cash so he wouldn't leave a paper trail of evidence. The last thing I wanted my mother to do was to find out that Lester had paid for a hotel room after opening a credit card statement. Then he'd have some explaining to do, and that wouldn't be good. He would have a room key and so would I, that way he could let himself into the hotel room without me being there. As for the Cadillac, he could park it behind the hotel or at the end of the parking lot.

After running this idea by Lester, he agreed with it one hundred percent. He said that he didn't mind paying because he would remember this for the rest of his life. That same day I went to the hotel to see the layout of the rooms. The hotel was rather new, but the closet doors looked to be refurbished. They resembled long shutters with thick slats, and they opened in a bi-fold manner. The peek-a-boo doors were perfect, and I was sure that Lester would be able to see through them.

While he was focused on getting his eyes full, I hoped that he remembered he had to pay me. He still didn't mention how much I would receive for pulling this off. I hoped it was at least three hundred bucks. I needed some more money to deposit into my bank account because my funds were getting low.

Two days later, Shay didn't have to work, so I sent Lester a text message and told him to pay for the room and leave a key at the front desk for me. He never responded, and I thought that he'd changed his mind. An hour later I messaged him again, and he responded right away. To my surprise, he was already there, and he said that he was setting up the room. I wanted to ask him what in the hell he was doing, but I didn't have time because Shay had been extra clingy today. She knew that my days of fun in the sun were coming to an end and that I would be leaving her soon.

When Shay took an important phone call about deejaying an event later this month, I put our bag of sex toys in the van along with an overnight bag prepared for the both of us. When I got back in the house, I told her that I had something special planned and asked her if it would be okay to blindfold her. She looked surprised and agreed to be blindfolded, and we got in the van. When we reached the hotel, I pulled our bags from the back of the van and walked around to the passenger side and opened Shay's door.

I guided her to a chair in the Lobby while I got the key from the lady at the front desk. Then we took the elevator up to the room. After I slid the key in the lock of the room door, I pushed it open and caught a glimpse of Lester as he darted into the closet. It was a good thing that her eyes were blindfolded or else he would have gotten caught. I almost cursed out loud, but kept the dirty word to myself as I looked around the room. It was beautiful, and I couldn't wait to yank the blindfold from her face so that she could see this too.

Lester had outdone himself. Candles were lit, slow jams from the mid-2000's were playing, rose petals were on the bed, and an ice bucket was stuffed with a bottle of champagne on the nightstand. After I had set the bags down on the small sofa near the bed, I asked Shay was she ready and untied the blindfold. The first thing that she saw was the rose petals; then she saw something that I had overlooked. Shot glasses on the counter with a tall bottle of Vodka and a tray of sliced strawberries.

"Oh my God! Summer you did all of this for me? How on earth did you do this? You've been with me all day."

I stammered as I answered, "Don't you worry about that."

"I knew that you loved me as much as I loved you. I'm so happy right now I could kiss you."

Without holding back, she moved in close and slipped her tongue between my lips. My knees felt a little weak as she wrapped her arms around my waist and a shiver went down my spine.

"Wait a minute. Let's take it slow. I'm going to start a shower for the both of us in a minute, let's crack open this champagne first."

"Alright," she said as she let me go and sat on the edge of the bed.

Before I opened the bottle of champagne, she suggested that we take a few shots of vodka instead. That was all right with me because I needed something to settle my nerves and I downed the shots quickly. I still couldn't stop thinking about Lester hiding in the closet as I headed into the bathroom. One wrong move and our cover would be blown.

Lester had candles and rose petals in the bathroom too. I couldn't wait to give him a high-five for a job well done. As I reached in to turn the shower on, I heard Shay say that she was going to put our things in the closet. My heart dropped as I came out to see that her hand was on one of the knobs to the closet door.

"No," I shouted as I snatched the bags from her and sat them back on the couch.

"What's wrong with you?"

"Nothing, I don't want you to lift a finger. Now can you please undress and meet me in the shower?"

"Oh, yeah. I can do that."

After Shay took off her shirt and threw it onto the couch, she went into the bathroom. My heart thumped inside of my chest as

I peeked inside the closet to check on Lester. He was sitting in the corner with a pillow, sheet, and a bottle of Gatorade. "Sorry about that, I'm going to keep her away from the closet," I whispered as Lester nodded his head okay.

Shay tried to seduce me in the shower. I gave in a little until I remembered that Lester was expecting a show in the bedroom. I bit my bottom lip and did my best to resist her advances, as I rinsed the suds from my body. When I turned the shower off and stepped out, Shay slapped me on my ass. I was shocked because it hurt like hell and it also turned me on. We chatted while we dried off and dropped our towels on the floor as we headed to the bed.

The first thing I did before I unzipped the bags on the couch was look at the closet door. I tried to act normal, but knowing that someone was watching me made me feel kind of shy. So I slowly pulled out a bottle of sweet smelling body oil, and tried not to look in the direction of the closet as I massaged the oil onto her skin. I made sure that I paid extra special attention to Shay's bubble butt and inner thighs.

After we were both oiled up, we had another shot of Vodka and fed fruit to one another. She sucked on my fingers as I teased her with the sweet ripe fruit. Then I opened the champagne and poured us each a glass. We sipped on the tart liquid slowly and were in each other's arms in no time. Now that the alcohol was in my bloodstream, I was a flaming ball of fire. I even poured champagne into Shay's navel and seductively lapped it out as she giggled.

I didn't know how Lester was feeling in the closet, but I knew that I felt like I was sick with a fever. I don't recall ever feeling this hot before, deep down I wondered if I was in love with Shay and felt guilty about Lester watching us. Only there was nothing I could do about it now, so I gave it all that I had.

I licked places that I'd never licked before. I couldn't get enough of her and begged her not to get out of the bed as she retrieved our bag of goodies off of the couch. The first thing that she pulled out was a clitoris stimulator. Without saying a word she turned the small purple device to the slow setting and positioned herself between my legs. At this moment, I felt like Shay and I didn't need to use any toys, but I quickly changed my mind when she placed the stimulator on the lips of my vagina and inserted her fingers.

I came within seconds and felt dizzy.

"Damn, baby that was fast. Let's see if you can go again," she said as she removed her fingers and sucked them.

I wanted to respond to her, but I couldn't, I was too weak and didn't know how much more of this I could take. When she dug into the bag of goodies the second time, I saw her pull out an eight-inch chocolate colored dildo and strap-on harness. I watched her step into the contraption and opened my legs a little wider as she climbed in between them. Her soft skin felt like a sheet of silk pressed against my body. Our nipples slightly rubbed against each other while she sucked and kissed the tender skin of my neck. Just as my juices started flowing, I palmed her ass, and the thick veiny dildo teased my opening.

I held my breath because I didn't know what to expect. I used this particular toy on her before, but she'd never used it on me. As the tip entered my wetness, I closed my eyes. When it was completely in, she kept a slow, but steady pace that hit all of the right spots. I relaxed more as she got into her rhythm, then the bed shook as she quickened her pace. I was wild with passion as she continued to make love to me.

I pulled her deeper inside as we kissed lustfully. I sucked her tongue and softly nibbled on her bottom lip while I released low sensual moans until I exploded. I couldn't contain my excitement and a stream of warm liquid escaped my vagina. Shay asked me if I was ready to stop and I told her no. As she kept pleasing me, I realized how realistic this felt and I wrapped my legs around her until I climaxed again.

I took long deep breaths while I lay on my back and watched her remove the harness. I slid closer to her as she got back on the bed and we cuddled. I almost drifted off when I remembered that Lester was in the closet, and I suggested that I run a bath for us. I didn't have any energy and didn't feel like moving a muscle, but I knew that Lester had to get out of here because it was getting late. "Do we have to?" She asked. "No, but it will be fun and relaxing." "I'm pooped; I'll agree to the bath if you promise to bathe me." "You got it," I replied as I got up and turned the water on in the bathtub.

Shay got in the tub while the water ran and asked for some strawberries and another glass of champagne. I happily fulfilled her request, but only after I opened the closet door to check on Lester.

"Is the coast clear?" He whispered.

"She's in the tub. I don't think that she'll get out but wait a few more minutes. I'll fake a sneeze when it's okay for you to make your exit. Don't forget to close the closet door back and text me when you get home."

Five minutes later, the tub was full of steamy water, bubble bath, and rose petals. As soon as I joined Shay, I faked a loud sneeze. The music was still playing, but I heard the door when it clicked to a close, and so did Shay.

"Was that the door?" She inquired as she leaned forward in the tub.

"I didn't hear anything," I lied.

"Maybe I've been drinking too much."

"Yeah, put that wine glass down and get over here. I'm supposed to be bathing you. Remember?"

After Lester left, Shay and I got wild in the bath tub. When we both got out, our fingers and toes were wrinkled like prunes. Before we got in bed to go to sleep, I turned the thermostat to a low setting and curled up next to her under a thin blanket. We talked for hours until she fell asleep. I drifted off and woke up in the middle of the night to use the bathroom. After I relieved my bladder, I checked my phone, and I had a missed call from Trevor and a text message from Lester. "Dammit," I whispered as I checked to see if Trevor had left a voice message. He didn't, so I opened the text message and read it silently.

"I just pulled up in the driveway, and I still have an erection. You don't know how bad I wanted to come out of that closet and whip my cock out on the two of you. That little dildo that y'all had wasn't nothing compared to what I could have given you. I enjoyed every minute of being in that closet, and I'm glad that you agreed to let me watch you. Come by the house tomorrow if you can and I'll pay you."

15

Clearing the Air

I couldn't believe that my summer vacation was coming to a close. I still hadn't made any contact with Trevor. He didn't leave a message the other night, so I had no idea where we stood relationship wise. I was still staying at Shay's, but mom wanted me to go to her house and start dinner because she had to help Bessie with some yard work. Imani was home, but she wasn't allowed to use the stove. My intentions were to go over, cook dinner, and get the hell out of there because I didn't want to see Lester. I didn't want the money that he was supposed to pay me. The entire situation made me sick to my stomach and I no longer wanted to hook up with him before I left to go back to Texas.

When Shay and I pulled into the driveway, I saw Lester's car parked and wondered why he couldn't start dinner. As I waved goodbye to Shay, I wished that she could stay here with me, but she had to check out a new club that she was going to be deejaying at this weekend. I let myself into the house and to my surprise, Lester or Imani was nowhere in sight. "Hello, is anybody home?" I called as I took my key out of the door and closed it.

I thought I was in the house alone until Lester came from down the hall.

"Hey, Summer. How's it going?"

"Hello, Lester. It's going well."

"Did that fine ass girlfriend of yours drop you off?"

"As a matter of fact, she did."

"I wish that she would have come in to say hello. I'd love to get a look at that nice round derriere."

I didn't want to hear him talking about her like that, so I changed the subject, and asked, "Where's Imani?"

"Oh, she's in her room listening to music."

"You know I could have cooked, but I told your mother to ask you if you would come by. Why didn't you respond to my text message the other night?"

"Look, I don't want to talk about that right now."

"Oh well, excuse me. I guess you don't want your money either then."

"I don't care Lester. If you want to pay me, pay me. If you don't, then don't."

After telling him exactly how I felt, I ignored Lester and bent down to look under the cabinet for a rice pot. When I felt his crotch on my rear end, I stood up, and he pulled me closer to him. Just as I turned around, he palmed my ass and slipped a few bills into the back pocket of my shorts.

"Will you back off? Imani is in the other room for crying out loud."

He took my advice and just in time because Imani turned the corner as soon as he backed away from me.

"Hey, Summer. I thought you were going to take me shopping for bras before you left. Can we go today?"

"As a matter of fact, we can go today. Do you mind if I drive your car, Lester?"

"No. I don't mind at all."

"Great," Imani yelled as she grabbed the keys from the hook by the front door.

With only the two of us left standing in the kitchen, Lester licked his lips and said, "I'll cook. Go ahead, have a good time."

"Thanks."

I headed out the door but quickly turned around when I remembered the blunt that was under the bathroom sink. In the bathroom, I shut the door and checked my back pocket to see how much money Lester had given me. I pulled two hundred dollar bills out and shoved the cash down in my bra before I started moving around the items that were under the sink. The blunt was nowhere in sight. I wondered if Imani smoked it. I wasn't sure, but I was going to find out today.

When I got to the car, I played it cool, until we pulled into the mall parking lot.

"I want to ask you a question, and I want you to answer if truthfully," I said as I parked, took off my seat belt, and turned towards Imani.

"A question about what?"

"A question about the blunt that was under the bathroom sink the last time that I came over. I just checked the cabinet before we left the house and it was gone."

Imani took a deep breath and looked out of the window before she answered, "I smoked it."

"Did you forget about the conversation that we had about weed before? Why would you do this to yourself?"

"I don't know. I won't do it again. That was the last of it. I swear."

"Since you already lied to me once, I don't believe you. If I find more weed in the house, I'm going to tell your father. Do you understand that?"

"Yeah, I understand."

After the conversation we had in the car about the weed, we carried on in the mall like it never happened. I bought Imani her first Victoria's Secret push up bra. She was excited to try it on in the fitting room. The bra was forty bucks, but it was worth it just to see her smile. Maybe if she felt better about herself, she wouldn't feel the need to smoke. Since I couldn't afford another bra from Victoria's Secret, we went to the nearest Wal-Mart and picked out six more bras. Of course, she chose bright colors and crazy patterns which were fine with me. She was the one that had to wear them.

The Hottest Summer

On the way back home Shay called me and said that she was at my mother's house waiting for me to get back. After I asked her if she was inside with Lester and she said that she was, I hightailed it back to the house. I didn't want Lester to make a move on her. I whipped the Cadillac through the streets of Miami like a hot knife through butter. My driving kind of reminded me of my mother's. Even though I was worried about Shay being alone with Lester, I gave Imani a few more reasons why she shouldn't smoke before we gathered her bags and went inside.

Before I could step on the porch, I smelled a mouth-watering aroma. I didn't know what Lester decided to cook, but it sure smelled good. After Imani turned the door knob and went right inside, I followed her, but instead of going down the hallway, I went into the kitchen. Shay was sitting at the table, and Lester was pulling something out of the oven. Shay greeted me as I pulled out the chair that was beside her.

"Any luck at the mall?" Lester asked.

"Yep. You shouldn't have to go bra shopping with Imani anytime soon. She tried all the bras on at the store, but she's probably in her room trying them on again."

"I appreciate you spending time with her, and I wish that you didn't have to go back home so soon."

"Yeah, can you stay for one more week?" Shay chimed in.

"I wish I could, but I can't. I've got a lot of things to get ready for. School starts back in three weeks, but I have to go back to work two weeks before the students come back. I'll have to attend several faculty meetings, prepare lesson plans, and I have to set up my classroom."

"Dang. I didn't know that you had to go through all of that." Shay said as she sipped lemonade through a straw.

"Yeah, it's a lot."

In the middle of our conversation, Imani entered the kitchen and asked me if I could come to her room for a second. Without asking why, I got up and went with her. I thought that she was going to ask me questions about the bras, but I was wrong. After we got to her room, she closed the door and went to her dresser drawer. Without saying a word, she handed me another small baggie of weed and two rolled blunts. As bad as I wanted to fuss, I didn't. I only took the drugs out of her hand and shoved them down into my pocket.

"That's it. I don't have anymore. I promise."

"Are you sure?"

"Yes, I'm positive. I don't want you to be mad at me, and I want you to come back and visit me."

"Imani, I'm going to come back and visit you. You know that you can call me anytime. Do you understand?"

"Yes. Summer I love you, and I'm glad that you're my sister."

My eyes watered as she stepped into my personal space and wrapped her skinny arms around my middle. We hugged for a minute, and I told her that I loved her as she rested her head on my chest. I didn't know it, but Imani was crying. When she let me go, I saw the tear stains on my shirt. They looked like rain drops.

After we had cleaned up our faces, I gave her another hug, and we went back into the kitchen with Shay and Lester. Mom had just walked in, so we all sat around the kitchen table and talked while Lester fixed us each a plate if BBQ pork chops, mac-n-cheese, and sweet corn on the cob. I'd never tasted pork chops like these before and was tempted to ask for the recipe, but I didn't. I would just ask Mark to make me some whenever I got back to Texas.

The night before I was due to leave we all hung out at Johaly's. The weather was perfect for a cookout. Without me knowing anything about it Johaly invited my mother and Lester to my going away party. I thought that Lester's eyes would pop out of his head when he saw me in my string bikini. I ended up changing into another one after I purposely spilled ketchup on my bikini top. I wish that would have she given me a heads up before inviting him. But then again why would she, she didn't have a clue that Lester and I had been intimate.

Even though things seemed a bit odd, my last night in Miami was great. As I looked around, I realized that this vacation was just what I needed in my life. I now had a better relationship with my mother, a little sister who looked up to me, a best friend, possibly a girlfriend, and a stepdad that has it going on.

When the party was over, I was torn between spending my last night with Imani, Johaly, or Shay. With all three of them pouting. We decided to have a sleepover at Johaly's. We watched movies and pigged out on junk food until Imani fell asleep. I still had the weed that she had given me the other day, and I gave it to Johaly and Shay.

After I covered Imani with a blanket, we went outside and put our feet in the shallow end of the pool.

While they enjoyed their personal blunts, I sat between the two of them and caught a contact high. I wasn't sure if I would need another one of those drinks from the vitamin shop, but I was going to get one in the morning just to be on the safe side. As the smoke made its way up my nostrils, my mind wandered to what life would be like in Texas without my friends, and I knew it was going to be dull.

Words couldn't describe how happy I was that I accepted my mother's invitation to visit. I was going to miss everyone, even the clerk at the gas station that always called me pretty lady. I wasn't ready to face reality and return to Texas, but I knew that I had to go. I had to go back to work and face Trevor and Mark.

16

Change is Good

Early the next morning, I booked my flight and packed my bags. Mom, Lester, Imani, Shay, and Johaly were sad to see me leave, but I had to get back into the swing of things and get all of this partying out of my system. Lester offered to take me to the airport, but I declined and let Shay take me instead. I knew that Lester giving me a ride wouldn't be a good idea because of what had happened between the two of us. I still couldn't believe that I had sex with my stepdad. This would definitely be a summer that I'd never forget.

After sharing a long kiss with Shay near the luggage check in, we hugged, and she even shed a tear before kissing and hugging me goodbye one final time. As soon as she left my side, I called Trevor to let him know that I was coming home, but I didn't get an answer. While I wondered where he was, I left a voice message and told him that I would be home by six this evening. I hope that he had his act together because I was ready for him to make a decision. If he wanted to marry me, I would marry him, but I honestly didn't have the same feelings towards him anymore.

Being with other people made me realize that Trevor wasn't the best catch. He was financially, but as far as sex, I knew that he wouldn't make me happy anymore. I knew that the wedding invitations were on the shelf in my bedroom, and I was secretly ready to toss them in the garbage. Since I told my mother what happened between the two of us, I didn't care what people thought if or when I told them that the wedding was canceled. That included the teachers at my school too. They all could kiss my ass, especially Mrs. Frye.

Being in Miami had opened my eyes to a whole new person that had been living on the inside of me. I'd changed; my nails and toes were painted in a vibrant hot pink color, my glasses were officially gone, I had blonde highlights, a caboodle full of makeup, and a sassy new attitude. I wasn't sure what Trevor was going to think about this, but there was only one way to find out.

On the plane, I sat between a lady with the cutest baby boy and a man who was engulfed in a paperback with the image of pink candied lips on the cover. I wanted to ask him about the novel, but I didn't want to interrupt him. I ended up reading the book description and wrote the name of the book down to check out on Google after I got settled in at home. I slept most of the flight until the baby started whining and wouldn't stop. I could tell that the mother was beyond frustrated so, I asked to hold the baby, and she gave him to me without hesitance. After bouncing the little fellow on my lap and making a few funny faces at him, he calmed down.

When I looked over to ask his mother did she want him back, I realized that she had fallen asleep. Since the baby was happy and quiet, I entertained him for the remainder of the flight and woke his sleeping mother up when the pilot was preparing to land. I startled her when I tapped her on the shoulder, and she woke up with a crazy look on her face.

"Ma'am, the plane is getting ready to land. Can you take your baby back now?" I asked in a whisper.

"Oh, I'm sorry. I was so sleepy. I couldn't resist drifting off," I apologize.

"That's okay. You have an adorable boy. I hope my kids are this cute when I have some."

"Thank you. Babies are cute, but they change your life. You look young. If I were you, I'd hold off on kids for another ten years or so because they're a pain in the ass. The older they get, the harder it is to raise them. Trust me; I know because I have a five-year-old and an eleven-year-old," she said as she reached in the baby bag and retrieved a pacifier.

"I hope I'm not being rude, but can I ask how old you are ma'am?"

"I guess I can tell you my age, considering that you babysat an hour for me," she replied with a laugh and then added, "I'm thirty-four."

"You look like you could still be in your twenties."

"Thank you. I can't believe that I got an uninterrupted nap and a compliment in the same day. I think I'll play the lottery tonight."

That was the end of our conversation. I never knew what the lady's name was or asked where her two other children were. As we lined up to get off of the airplane, the lady put her purse, carry-on bag, and diaper bag straps on one shoulder, and put her adorable son on her hip. The baby watched me with his crystal blue eyes until his mother ducked into a restroom in the airport, and I never saw the two of them again.

While I waited for my luggage at the baggage carousel, I wondered how the lady was going to handle the rest of her luggage and manage carrying the baby. *"Maybe someone was going to meet her here,"* I thought as I saw my bags getting closer to my grasp. After I had taken my luggage off of the conveyor belt, I saw a navy blue baby stroller next to an enormous red suitcase. As it continued to make its way around the carousel, I knew that the stroller belonged to the lady with the baby. Now that my mind was at ease, I pulled out my cell phone and called Trevor again. I still didn't get an answer, and this bothered me.

When I reached my car, I popped the trunk and put my bags inside. Just as I started the engine and pulled out the airport parking lot, my cell phone rang. Thinking that it was Trevor calling, I quickly answered the call. To my surprise, it was Mark. The past few days had been so crazy that I didn't get a chance to call and tell him that I was coming back home today. Considering that I didn't know how this whole thing was going to play out with Trevor yet, I played it cool.

"Hello," I answered.

"How's it going?"

"It's going well. I'm back in Texas. I just left the airport."

"I can't wait to see you. Do you think that we can have dinner tomorrow night? I get off work at six."

"Are you working at the grocery store today?" I asked as I passed by and skimmed the parking lot for his truck.

"No, I'm working at the police station, and you didn't answer my question about dinner yet."

"I think I'll be all settled in by tomorrow afternoon, and dinner sounds like a plan. I actually need to talk to you about something," I confessed.

"I hope it's something good."

I briefly paused because I wasn't sure if I was going to deliver good news or bad news tomorrow at our dinner date, and changed the subject.

"Will you be cooking or are we going out? I think Applebee's has a two for $20 deal."

"Two for $20, are you serious?" He chuckled and then added, "We will not be going to Applebee's. I'd like to cook dinner for you at my place, and I need to talk to you about something as well."

My heartbeat quickened when he mentioned asking me a question. I wonder what he wanted to ask or tell me. *"Could he be gay or possibly engaged also?"* After talking with Mark for a few more minutes, he ended the call because his break was over. For the rest of the ride home, my stomach growled as I remembered the meal that Mark cooked at my place before I left to go to Miami.

When I reached the Penelope Terrace sign at the entrance of my apartment complex, I pulled into a space and put the car in park. Before I looked for Trevor's car, I text messaged Mom, Johaly, and Shay to let them know that I had made it home safely. After I had pressed send, I looked up and immediately noticed that Trevor's car was parked near my apartment. The wheels in my head turned as I grabbed my purse from the passenger seat and got out of the car. As I walked to my apartment door, I smelled food cooking. *"How could an aroma be coming from my apartment?"* I asked myself. I had gotten the locks changed before I left so, Trevor shouldn't have been able to get in. When I got closer to the door, I heard talking coming from inside. Instead of standing on the outside wondering what in the hell could be going on, I inserted my key into the knob; only to find out that it didn't work.

I eased the key inside of the knob again, and nothing happened. I knew that the key worked because I unlocked this door with this same key before I left to go to Miami. *"Was this the right apartment?"* I thought as I stepped back and looked at the letter and number on the door. I saw "3B", this was the correct apartment. After trying my key again, I was left with no other option. I had to knock on the door. Before I knocked the first time, I took a deep breath because I didn't know what I was about to walk into. I heard a lady's voice from the other side of the door, and I backed up a little.

When she swung the door open, she said, "Can I help you?" My mouth got dry as I peered over her shoulder and saw that everything looked different in my apartment.

"I'm looking for a woman by the name of Summer," I lied.

"I think that was the chick that used to live here. She got evicted or something. I live here now," she blurted, with an attitude.

"Oh, I'm sorry for interrupting your meal, but do you think that I could use your bathroom before I go?"

I thought that I was about to get punched by the look on the woman's face, but I guess she had a soft heart because she let me in.

"Sure, it's right down that hallway," she pointed and headed back into the kitchen.

I looked around as I entered my old apartment. An overweight man who looked to be in his forties was relaxing in a reclining chair in the corner. While he smoked a cigarette, he watched an action packed movie and shouted out things like, *shoot his ass, get out of the way,* and *run,* as I headed down the hallway. I paid him no attention as I saw how different everything looked. The walls were even painted a different color. Knowing good and well that the door I was about to open wasn't the bathroom, I opened it anyway.

I peeked inside of my old bedroom to see nothing familiar. Not only were all of Trevor's things gone, but my things were gone as well. After I'd seen enough, I shut the door quietly and used the bathroom in the hall, like I initially asked the woman to do. Without thinking, I sat down on the toilet. While I only urinated, my stomach started to cramp, and I released gas into the toilet bowl. My nerves were getting the best of me, and I couldn't fight the urge any longer.

I took a crap in the unfamiliar bathroom that used to be so familiar to me and cleaned myself up. After flushing the toilet, I looked under the cabinet and sprayed some air freshener. Then I washed my hands, turned the fan on, and closed the bathroom door. I checked the other room that Trevor and I used as a home office, and it now belonged to a teenage girl. Complete with purple covers and a shelf full of CDs. After getting one final peek, I walked back into the living room and thanked the woman for her hospitality. "No problem. Would you like something to eat? I could fix you a plate if you'd like." It was true. I was hungry, and I didn't know this lady from a can of paint, but I'd seen her entire apartment, and it was clean as a whip. So without hesitation, I accepted her offer and waited patiently as she fixed me a plate to go.

My mouth watered as she filled the paper plate with dry yellow rice, collards, pork chop smothered in gravy, and corn bread. "Thank you," I said as I walked across the threshold of the apartment. "You're welcome if you're ever in the neighborhood again feel free to stop by. We're new to Texas, and I don't have any friends yet." "Alright," I said as I waved to her.

When I reached the parking lot, I set the plate on the hood of my car and walked over to Trevor's car. After I had looked inside I saw a car seat buckled in the back seat, then I checked the license plate and realized that the tag number was different. This wasn't Trevor's car. Without thinking, I walked down the sidewalk to the young lady's apartment that I had seen Trevor with. After pounding on the door for five minutes, no one ever answered. I wasn't sure if she was home and afraid to come out, so I pressed my face up to the window and saw that the apartment was empty. No furniture was anywhere in sight. I guess she had moved.

Since I had nowhere to go, I went to a nearby hotel and checked in. Thanks to Trevor I was officially homeless. I crossed my fingers as I called him three more times and hoped he answered, but he didn't. I was beyond furious and wanted to knock his head off of his shoulders. Maybe this was the confirmation that I needed to distance myself from him. I'd talked to him while I was in Miami and I thought that we were cool, I guess after I missed all of his calls he thought that I wanted to move on. Whatever the case, I had no clue that he didn't renew the lease on the apartment. By the looks of things, I knew that he'd made his narrow mind up, and there wasn't going to be a wedding for us in the spring.

It was time for me to figure things out all by myself. I lay on the bed in the hotel room while the muted television went to a commercial break. When I saw a man in a police uniform, I thought about Mark. I wanted to talk to him more than ever, but he was at work, and I didn't want to bother him with my troubles. Besides, how do you tell your new love interest that you're homeless? I had a week to get my shit together before I had to go back to work, and I couldn't let thoughts about Trevor, Mark, or whoever deter me from doing that.

After I took a hot shower and ate the food that the woman had fixed, I got the phone book out and wrote down all the numbers to apartment complexes that I could find. I knew that there was an apartment available at Penelope Terrace, but I didn't want to live in the same apartment that Trevor's new girlfriend had lived in.

That next morning I called all the complexes that were within a ten-mile radius of the school I worked at. Out of the nine complexes, only three of them had vacancies. After filling my belly with the complimentary hotel breakfast, I stopped by the first complex. It looked nice and was on the higher end of my budget at nine hundred bucks a month. This place was called Carolina Village, and it was just as beautiful as my old apartment at Penelope Terrace except there was only one bedroom.

The next set of apartments was a vibrant red brick color on the outside and was called Tara Acres. I liked the two bedroom apartment, but it was upstairs, and I didn't want to climb stairs on a daily basis. Even though this place was only an extra hundred bucks per month and had an extra room, I had to pass on this one. The last apartment complex that I looked at was covered with white siding. This place was across the street from the high school and was called Country Club Oaks. It was almost as nice as my old place, and it was on the bottom floor. The rent was only seven hundred dollars a month, and there was no gym or pool. I could live without a pool and a gym, so this place was perfect for me, and I decided to start the paperwork for this apartment.

After the lady in the office checked my credit. She ran my debit card for the payment of the first and last month's rent. I mentally deducted the fourteen hundred bucks from my bank account and was happy as ever when she handed over the keys. This was a new beginning for me. I'd never lived alone, and I was proud of myself for taking this step without being a complete basket case. I could make it without Trevor and his bill money.

After I received my keys, I went back to my new apartment. This one was apartment "5C". It was towards the back of the complex, and that was fine with me. I wanted to live closer to my job, but I didn't want to see it as soon as I opened my front door. Everything checked out okay, and I opened the windows before I left to let some fresh air in.

Before I went back to the hotel to check out and get the rest of my things. I stopped by the light company and the water company. I had to dish out more money, but that was okay because I knew that nobody could put me out of my own place. With my debit card begging me not to use it again today, I stopped by a Walmart and purchased a blow-up mattress, a few personal items, and a blanket.

I pulled it off. I was in a new place, and I did it all without having to cancel my date with Mark tonight. That reminded me that all I had were the clothes that were in my suitcase, and they were quite scandalous. I couldn't wear them around here. Some of the kids may see me from school. After I took a deep breath, I called to check my account balance. All I had was six hundred dollars left.

With so little money, I knew that I couldn't afford to get new clothes, and I didn't want to call my mother for money. It looked like my only option was to go on a shopping spree at the Goodwill or the Salvation Army. The nearest resale shop was only a few minutes away, so I drove there and crossed my fingers that I could find some clothes in my size.

The Goodwill was packed with shoppers. There were rows and rows of clothing, and everything was color coordinated. I checked out the ladies section first, and I found several pairs of slacks, three cardigans, and six dress shirts. After I had a week's worth of work clothes in my buggy, I shopped for jeans. I was lucky enough to find two pairs, and I headed to the checkout.

When I reached my apartment, I washed all the clothes that were from the Goodwill and the ones that were packed in my suitcase. At this moment I knew I had selected the correct apartment because it came with a washer and a dryer already installed. After the day I had, the last thing I wanted to do was sit inside of a laundromat. My apartment smelled like fields of lavender while my last load of clothes tumbled around in the dryer.

I looked around my new place with a gigantic smile on my face. Even though my wedding invitations were long gone, so were my feelings for Trevor. I started to go to his job and make a scene, but some things just aren't worth the time and energy. I'd already given him ten years of my life. I wasn't going to waste another second thinking about him and how bad he did me.

As I put Trevor out of my head for good, I wondered what Mark wanted to ask me while I got ready for our date. I wanted to talk to him about the engagement that I was in, but since I'm not engaged anymore, I'm decided that I wasn't even going to bring that up. It wasn't important anymore. I dressed in a tight pair of Levi's and a low cut cream striped blouse. The shirt matched my contacts as well as a pair of wedge sandals that I purchased when I was in Miami.

Before I walked out the door, Mark called to give me directions. While he told me how to get to his place, I realized that he lived in one of the complexes that I visited earlier today. As I pulled into a parking space, I thanked God that I chose another complex because that would have been awkward.

I ended the call with him when I saw him coming down a staircase with a bouquet of flowers and a dimpled smile. I licked my lips as I got out of my car and walked towards him. We shared a long hug, and then he handed me the flowers.

"It's so good to see you. I missed you like crazy."

I smiled as I replied, "I missed you too."

"I hope you're hungry," he said as he reached for my hand and walked me to the stairs that led to his apartment.

I could smell the aroma of the food from the bottom of the stairs and asked, "Did you cook lasagna?"

"Man. You have a good sense of smell. That's exactly what I made."

We both giggled as we walked up the stairs and entered his apartment. The lights were dim, and candles were lit. My eyes focused on a bottle of champagne that was sitting on the counter. It was the same kind that Lester had in the hotel room back in Miami. I smiled to myself as he showed me around the one bedroom apartment and led me back to the kitchen.

"What did you want to ask me?" I blurted.

"Can this wait until after dinner?"

"Please don't make me wait any longer," I begged.

After taking a deep breath, he replied, "Alright. I'm really digging you. I wanted to ask if you'd consider being my girlfriend. I know that we haven't known each other that long, but I feel like we could have something real."

After thinking about his question for a second, I answered, "I'd be honored to."

Mark bent down and gave me a kiss on the lips and then asked, "Now what was it that you wanted to tell me?"

I froze as I thought about the whole Trevor thing and said, "Oh, I only wanted to tell you that I moved. I live in the apartments across from the high school."

"Oh, I thought it was something else. You had me shaking in my boots for nothing."

I laughed it off as he popped the top off of the champagne and we had our first drink as a couple. After he pulled my chair out, he served dinner, and we talked about my trip to Miami. Of course, I didn't tell him about sleeping with Manny, Lester, and Shay. I kept that to myself. I did tell him about Imani and the weed, my mother's bingo obsession, and the new house. Then I asked him about his new job at the police station.

We talked for hours and ended up drinking the entire bottle of champagne. I was going to go home, but he insisted that I stay the night. He was a perfect gentleman and didn't get fresh with me at all. We ended up talking until I fell asleep in his arms.

———•——•—•———

The weeks passed by quickly and I hadn't heard a word from Trevor. I know that I said that I wasn't worried about him, but I wanted an explanation about the whole apartment situation. I was puzzled and couldn't wait to bump into him somewhere around town, but I hadn't seen him or his car. Only cars that looked like his caught my attention in parking lots and on the highways as I drove. I called his job and asked to speak to him, and his secretary put me on hold for almost an hour. That was the day that I decided to give up on getting an apology. Obviously, he didn't want anything to do with me, and his previous actions showed me that he didn't give a damn.

Mark and I were getting to know each other better, I know that we'd only met a few months ago, but the connection between the two of us was unbelievable. He seemed perfect, and he hadn't even made a move on me yet. We only kissed and held hands a lot. I wondered what was up with him, but I didn't let it bother me too much because I wanted to take things slow. I moved fast enough while I was in Miami and needed this break.

The first day of school had finally arrived, and I had to admit that I was a little excited. All of my things were laid out for the day, and I was ready to teach. Before I walked to work, I called my mother to tell her good morning. She asked if I needed anything and I let her know that I was okay before I asked to speak to Imani. My mother yelled for her to come to the phone when I heard Lester's voice in the background. My soul quivered as I thought about the sex that we had. I sincerely regretted it, but I would always remember my encounters with him.

"Hey Summer," she said as she got on the phone.

"Hey, how's it going?"

"It's going great."

"Are you excited about school starting back?"

"Yeah, I am. I can't wait to tell everyone about my cool big sister."

"Aw, that's so sweet. You make sure you stay away from that weed too. I'll call you this evening to see how your day went."

Imani let out a giggle and said, "You got it. Hey Summer, do you think that you can come back to visit for Christmas or Thanksgiving?"

"I may be able to come for Christmas."

"Okay. I love you. I hope that you have a good first day of school too."

"I love you too, Imani. Thank you."

After I hung up the phone with Imani, I pressed the button at the crosswalk and waited for the light to change before I crossed the street. I burst out laughing as I thought about how her face looked when I caught her with that weed in the bathroom. I hope that the little knucklehead learned a lesson and wouldn't try to smoke again. As I entered the office, the secretary gave me a double-take and said, "Look at you. Summer you look amazing. I love your lime green nail polish too." "Thank you," I replied as I signed in and made my way down the hallway.

"Young lady, students are not allowed in the school building until 7:45," A voice echoed. I continued to walk until the voice repeated itself and I turned around to see Mrs. Frye. Considering that we were the only two people in the hallway, I knew that she had to be talking to me.

"Ms. Barnes, is that you?" She asked as she walked a little closer.

"Yes, Mrs. Frye. It's me."

"My goodness, you look so young. I thought you were a student. What did you do to your hair and where are your glasses?"

"Thank you. I got some highlights, and I started wearing contacts over the summer vacation."

"Well, you look great. It's still Ms. Barnes isn't it? You didn't have your wedding yet did you?"

"Yes, it's still Ms. Barnes," I answered with clenched teeth.

"I hope you have a good first day. Don't forget that you have lunch duty today," she said as she walked away to harass another teacher.

"Whatever," I said under my breath as I walked to my classroom door and unlocked it.

I had a few minutes before the bell rang so, I primped in the mirror and checked my phone for text messages. A good morning text from Shay made my face light up, and I messaged her a few times before my day started. As she messaged how much she missed me, the bell sounded, and I put my phone away. I thought of her lying in bed with a sheet wrapped around her nude body as students that I'd never seen before poured into my class. Naughty thoughts entered my mind as the students stood up for the Pledge of Allegiance and morning announcements. Then they settled into their seats once again, and I stood up to introduce myself to them.

"My name is Mrs. Barnes. I don't have time for any of your games or foolish behavior. When you enter this classroom, come correct, and be prepared to work. Please sit quietly as I pass out copies of your syllabus and a list of required items you'll need for this class," I said with a straight face.

Before I turned around to grab a stack of handouts off my desk, one of the boys raised his hand and asked, "Mrs. Barnes, how was your summer?" I knew that this student was already trying to get me off task, and I started not to answer him, but I couldn't resist. "Oh, it was pretty hot."

To Be Continued...